The Seventh Handmaiden

Judith Pransky

Green
Bean
Books

Green Bean Books

First published in 2020 by Green Bean Books,
c/o Pen & Sword Books Ltd,
47 Church Street, Barnsley, S. Yorkshire, S70 2AS
www.greenbeanbooks.com

ISBN 978-1-78438-589-7

Library of Congress Cataloging-in Publication Data available

Typeset by JCS Publishing Services Ltd, www.jcs-publishing.co.uk
Printed and bound by CPI Group (UK) Ltd, Croydon, CR0 4YY

Dedicated to the teachers who inspired my love of learning and exploring the past; and the students whose comments and questions kept reminding me that there is always more to discover

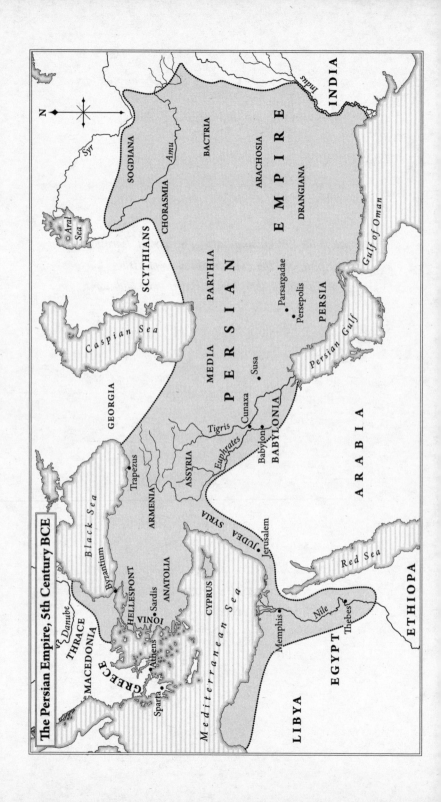

The Persian Empire, 5th Century BCE

Acknowledgements

It took years to write and revise this novel and finally have it win the Association of Jewish Libraries Manuscript Award. This led to its inclusion in the PJ Our Way list and its acceptance by Green Bean Books. Many people were involved, and all of them deserve my heartfelt thanks for reading, commenting, suggesting, guiding, and encouraging:

- My extended family, first and foremost—especially my mother-in-law Ruth, whose insightful remarks changed the course of the narrative; and my granddaughter Tzipporah (and friends), whose enthusiasm buoyed my hopes of finding a publisher
- Altie Karper, editorial director of Schocken Books, for indispensable advice
- Publishing consultants Anne Dubuisson and Paula Breen
- Middle school director Chris Farrell and phenomenal teacher Leslie Pugach for invaluable input
- Extraordinary school librarian Wendie Sittenfield, who encouraged me to submit the manuscript to the AJL and introduced me to—
- Adena Potok, whose support and belief in the novel were beyond measure

- The AJL team, especially committee chair Aileen Grossberg
- The PJ Our Way team, especially director Catriella Freedman
- And, of course, publisher Michael Leventhal and his excellent team at Green Bean Books, in particular project manager Jessica Cuthbert-Smith, whose meticulous work and professionalism are much appreciated. Thanks also to Saray Garcia Rua for the captivating artwork that graces the cover of the novel, and to Peter Wilkinson for his clear and precise cartography.

Finally, no words can express my gratitude to my husband for fully supporting this endeavor and all I have ever tried to accomplish.

Prologue
Persia, 485 BCE

The woman heard the children before she saw them, and the sound of their carefree laughter clawed at her heart.

Do not look at them, she warned herself, standing in the kitchen vegetable garden. *It will only make things worse. Collect the eggplant and carrots you came here for, and take yourself back into the kitchen to prepare the stew for the master's dinner.*

But almost as though they were acting on their own, her feet stepped toward the wooden trellis that screened the kitchen from a formal garden. She peered through the trellis and was struck as always by the breathtaking beauty on the other side. The walled garden was truly a paradise. Overhead, a mosaic of green leaves and turquoise sky gleamed like polished tiles on this perfect summer day. Underfoot, white pebbled walkways curled through a carpet of grass and flowers that looked as though it had been patterned on a magic loom.

And there were the young children she had heard—two girls and two boys. The boys captured her attention first, because they were taller and louder and never seemed to stop moving. In knee-length tunics and close-fitting trousers, they chased each other along the paths, leaped over small shrubs in the grass, and picked up pebbles to aim at the tree trunks. The girls were smaller and stood close together, holding hands, watching the boys with wide eyes. Playful ribbons and matching patterned tunics over colorful pantaloons set off their flawless skin and dark hair and made the girls seem like part of the flowering garden. Their musical voices blended with the cooing of palm doves nesting in the trees.

The woman behind the trellis stared at the entrancing little girls, looking from one to the other and back again. Slowly, her eyes widened with the realization that the girls were so identical that one of them could have been standing next to an image of herself in a mirror.

Two the same—twins, the woman murmured, *while I will no longer have even a single child. She will be taken from me and sold to slave dealers!* Her mouth contorted in bitterness and pain as tears welled up in her eyes. She tried to turn away but could not. Her gaze was riveted on the girls while she absently twisted the coarse fabric of the large, empty vegetable sack in her hands.

As the woman watched, the boys tired of their running and shouting. They wanted to play a game of hiding and seeking with the girls. The girls shook their heads, but the boys were insistent. While the older boy faced a tree trunk and covered his eyes, the three younger children cast about for hiding places. Giggling, the two girls ran together behind a bush of flaming orange hibiscus, but the younger boy rushed after them, hissing at them to separate before he hurried off to find his own place. The girls' smiles faded as, reluctantly, they let go of each other's hands and moved apart. Separated, they looked forlorn and vulnerable. While one stayed behind the flowering bush, the other searched for a new hiding place. She ran behind a tree, but the trunk was not thick enough to shield her, so she crouched behind a rose bush, which she realized was not high enough. Then she spied the trellis and rushed toward it, bounding into the vegetable garden just as the watching woman stepped into the shadows behind the open kitchen doorway.

The woman could hear the child's panting and see the tension in the tiny shoulders as the little girl crouched and peered through the trellis. The ribboned dark hair reminded the woman so much of her own daughter that fresh tears filled her eyes.

Why do you torment me? she pleaded silently to the gods, raising one hand to finger an amulet around her neck. *Why did you bring this child here to rub salt in my wounds?* But her own words struck her. The gods had certainly brought the child there!

Did you bring her to me for a reason? she asked them silently. *Dear* Ahura Mazda *and all the* ahura—*gods of goodness and light—are you not taunting me, but trying to help somehow?* She had prayed so hard and so tearfully for help. All of the *ahura* knew how much pain she endured. *What do you want of me?* she implored. *Why was this child brought close to me in this garden? Dear* ahura, *show me the way. Give me a sign.*

And then her eyes caught sight of the second little girl on the other side of the trellis. It was a sign! It had to be! Why else would this child have a double, a twin to salve her parents' hearts if she were gone? The woman knew she could never leave another parent bereft as she was—empty and grieving. But these parents would still have someone to love, another child to shower with care, if this one were taken.

No. She could not believe that the *ahura* were telling her to do something so terrible. How could she be so cruel as to kidnap a child? But how could she not? She had to present a small girl to the slave dealers, and if there were none other, it would be her own daughter—her own beloved daughter being sold to them!

Dear ahura, she prayed silently, clutching her amulet. *Help me. Please help me! I do not belong to the* daeva, *lords of darkness and evil. I belong to you. Help me know what to do. Help me save my child.*

One

Six Years Later

Darya awoke in the pre-dawn darkness. As always, she stretched out her arms on either side of her body and looked quickly toward the dark square of window, searching for glimmers of light that promised sunrise. She needed this morning ritual, this stretching and searching for light, because she always awoke with the dread that she was locked in a small, dark space, and she needed to reassure herself that this was not so. Jaleh, the housekeeper, indulged her by not closing the shutters completely at night, so that from her straw mat on the floor Darya could glimpse the moon and stars as she fell asleep and the first rays of light as she awoke.

Dear Jaleh, Darya thought fondly, looking toward the shadowy mound that was the housekeeper's soft pallet against the wall of the small room. *And dear Parvaneh. How would I survive without them?* Darya could hear the measured breathing of the woman and her eleven-year-old daughter, still asleep together. When she was younger, Parvaneh had often shared Darya's mat on the floor, the two of them curled up together like a pair of kittens. But now Parvaneh preferred to sleep on her mother's pallet, stuffed with feathers and goose down that Jaleh had salvaged from the kitchen.

Darya missed her friend's close proximity through the dark nights, and at first found it difficult to fall asleep alone on the floor. She felt as though a part of her were missing when Parvaneh moved to the pallet, as though she needed another person within reach to feel complete. These were feelings she did not understand, just as she did not fully comprehend her morning terrors.

Jaleh was certain their cause lay somewhere in the part of her life that Darya could not remember clearly. That time was almost as dark and shrouded as the realm of the *daeva*: the time before Darya was bought by her master, the army captain, as a slave for Monir, his small daughter.

The earliest clear memory Darya could ever call forth in her mind was the day she stood trembling in the crowded slave market of Susa, one of the splendid capitals of the great Persian Empire, tied to four older children: three boys with the dark skin of Nubia and a girl from the barbarian north, with sun-yellow hair and sky-blue eyes. Of course, Darya knew nothing of Nubia or barbarians back then; after all, she was only five or six years old at the time. She remembered staring fearfully at the other children's skin and hair and eyes, wondering what sort of strange beings they were, until her attention was diverted by the people who had come to buy slaves.

"Stand straight and stop shaking!" the slave dealer had ordered, grabbing Darya's shoulders to pull her erect before his customers. "And may the *daeva* take you if you do not stop your crying!" he added, as tears began streaming down

Darya's face. "Who will want to buy a girl who always cries?" He stepped away from her to scan the marketplace, looking for customers, but kept muttering angrily.

"It is enough that you wasted a moon's worth of my time nursing you back to health after I bought you. Those cheating dealers swore you were as healthy as all the other slaves in their caravan, that they kept you in that box on the wagon to make sure you were not stolen since you were so small, but they were lying through their broken teeth. Now it is time for me to get my money's worth."

Darya bit her lip and wiped her face with her hands. She had no clear recollection of the slave caravan or of being sick. Instead, she sensed a jumble of sounds and smells and feelings, all shrouded in inky darkness. For weeks that seemed to have gone on forever, her body had sweated with unbearable heat, then shivered uncontrollably with icy chills. Her mouth had been intensely dry as she lay in the small, dark space on the slave dealer's wagon. Her head and arms had felt too heavy to lift, while her legs had seemed devoid of strength, light enough to float on air.

She had dreamed of beautiful people, a man and woman, smiling at her and speaking kindly and soothingly, and a playful little girl, holding her hand; but when she opened her eyes, all was black, and the only voices she heard were harsh and cruel. Her dream land was airy and as spacious as the heavens, but the black space surrounding her was tight and close, leaving her no room to stretch her limbs. And in her dream world she ate fruits and cakes and sweets at tables laid with painted dishes; but in the blackness, foul-tasting food and drink were placed beside her in the box by hands she could barely see.

She vaguely recalled being lifted from the darkness by a new slave dealer and screaming when he ordered that buckets of cold water be poured over her to wash her. Then, terrified, she was handed over to a giant blacksmith who fashioned a narrow iron collar that lay loose and heavy around her neck. Later, in a dark hut, the slave dealer hammered a long chain to the back of the collar and fastened it to an iron ring set into the stone wall. And that was where Darya was tethered until the chills and sweats abated.

She was afraid of this new slave dealer from the start, with his *kulah*, his tall black felt hat, perched on his unruly hair, and his dark-green tunic smelling of garlic and soiled with drippings from his meals. He was a short, round man, who had poked the five children awake that morning, then doused all of them with his buckets of cold water to clean the sweat and grime that was caked on their skin. The yellow-haired girl and the dark-skinned boys had cried out with words Darya did not understand, but quieted when the dealer handed them clay bowls heaped with barley and beans so they would be well fed when he displayed them at the slave market. Darya had only stared at the food through her tears while the other children stuffed handfuls into their mouths.

"No crying!" he had ordered that morning as well, while he tugged a comb through her dark, wavy hair. "Not if you want the *ahura* to shine their light on you. They will make sure you are bought by a good family that will treat you well, instead of some workhouse that will use you to collect animal droppings for farmers' fields. But you must stop crying, eat, and look your best. You speak Aramaic, which makes you worth more than these foreigners you are tied to, so do not ruin your chances—or mine," he muttered.

Darya remembered his words as she stood in the market and tried her hardest to stand straight and quench her tears. She watched as men and women fingered the older girl's yellow hair and looked into her eyes, marveling at their color, while the girl hunched over to hide from their stares, and the dealer kept ordering her to stand upright.

Other customers prodded the boys' arms and legs, trying to gauge their strength. Very few buyers glanced at Darya, the smallest of the group, even when the dealer repeatedly advertised that she spoke Aramaic and proclaimed that the youngest slaves were the best since they could be trained more easily.

After four hours of baking in the heat under the dealer's linen awning, only Darya remained unsold. The yellow-haired girl was bought first, by two men who had moved from dealer to dealer, buying all the exotic-looking girls on the market to train as dancers. Then the boys were sold, one of them to a stonemason and two to labor in a copper mine.

"It is too hot to stay here any longer," the dealer grumbled, struggling up from where he had been reclining on brightly colored cushions. He had ordered the children to carry them to the market for him in the morning and pile them in a comfortable stack on the ground. Starting to take down his awning, he muttered, "Buyers are looking for a cool place to eat lunch, not for slaves."

Darya realized this meant she would be led back to the dark, dank room where she had awakened that morning, and that she would be chained to the wall alone, without even the foreigners for company. She wanted to cry again, but instead looked desperately around the marketplace, hoping more buyers were coming her way. The dealer was right: only a handful of prospects were still there, and other dealers were also taking down their awnings.

At a stall nearby stood a man in a spotless white tunic and trousers, holding the hand of a little girl younger than Darya. They were examining a slave girl, and Darya could hear the man discussing her price with her dealer. But when his child tugged at his sleeve and shook her head, the two of them turned away and slowly came toward Darya.

The little girl was well cared for, with a colorful dress and ribboned hair. The way her father held her hand protectively made Darya feel forlorn and almost brought tears to her eyes again, reminding her as it did of the beautiful man and woman in her dreams, but she forced herself to stand straight and smile shyly. The little girl smiled back and stepped closer. "What is your name?" she asked softly in Aramaic.

Darya stood tongue-tied for a moment, searching her blank mind for a name that sounded familiar.

"She is called Darya," the dealer put in helpfully, coming up behind Darya and placing his hands possessively on her shoulders. *Darya?* she questioned silently. The name sounded strange. But she had no time to wonder about it, because the dealer was leaning toward the well-dressed child, attempting a friendly smile. "A good Persian name— even if we do not know where she is from." He looked up at the child's father, the smile still plastered across his face. "And she speaks Aramaic, which will make her an excellent slave. Worth every gold *daric* you would pay for her."

"My name is Monir," the child said, barely audibly, looking from Darya's face to her body clothed in rags. Slowly, she unwound a long, pink, gossamer shawl from around her shoulders and handed it to Darya, who gratefully took it and let the dealer drape it about her with a satisfied grunt.

A pleased expression spread across the army captain's face above his combed and curled beard. It seemed he had finally found the right slave for his daughter.

Two

That is as far back as I can remember with any certainty, Darya thought now, rising from her mat on the floor and padding quietly from the room so as not to disturb Jaleh and Parvaneh. Whatever her life had been before the confused days in the slave caravan, wherever she had come from, whoever her family was, whoever had named her, however she had become the property of slave dealers—all that was shrouded in mystery, heaped into an impenetrable tangle of nightmares, bright dreams, terror, and illness, so that she could not sort out what was real and what was fevered imagining. The truth was hidden behind a dark, impassable wall in her mind.

When she had awakened tied to the other children the morning of her sale, her mind had been a confused turmoil, churning and roiling like an angry sea. And when it finally quieted, after the captain had bought her for Monir, it gradually grew blank and still, muffling all memories; now it was clear, smooth, and empty as freshly washed sands on the shore.

Darya knew she had been lucky six years ago to have been bought to serve Monir. The girl was two years younger, the only child of the army captain, who had been widowed when his daughter was born. He had been looking for more than a slave that day in the market; he wanted a playmate for his cherished child, a companion for the many times he was away from home. So Darya not only cleaned Monir's room and cared for her needs; she also played games with her, traveled around Susa with her and her father or tutor, learned to paint and embroider with her, and much more.

Most wonderfully, to Darya's mind, she learned to read and write along with Monir. It was almost unheard of in Susa for girls to be taught such things. Indeed, in all of Persia, only select boys were chosen to formally learn the short Aramaic alphabet or the far more complicated Persian wedge writing.

"Not even King Xerxes himself has ever wasted time learning to read and write," friends told Monir's father. "He has scribes to read his royal messages and create all those kingly papyrus scrolls. And masons chisel his proclamations in stone."

Monir's father only smiled and ignored their arguments. He had traveled the world with the King's army and was convinced that reading and writing gave people an advantage. "She is my only child and this is something I want for her," he insisted. "After all, she might need it someday. What if I am not here to protect her and provide for her, and she is not yet married? She might need to run the household or a business, and to know what a contract says."

And thus, Monir began gaining the skill of reading and writing, and her slave was present at the lessons as well.

At first, Darya was there merely to attend to her young mistress's needs, but when the tutor realized Darya was actually paying attention and learning the lessons, he began using her to help Monir with her studies. Darya treasured the sessions with Monir's tutor, marveling at the miracle of being able to decipher the letters or the wedge marks he made with a sharp reed on his clay tablet.

And she knew she was lucky two- and three-fold when Jaleh was hired as housekeeper and cook only a few months after Darya was purchased, joining the household with her daughter Parvaneh. The woman who had been there before Jaleh had no patience for Darya.

"Lazy dog!" the first housekeeper had muttered, poking Darya awake the morning after she was sold to the army captain, as the slave dealer had done. "No fire in the hearth! Nothing prepared! Dear gods, yesterday's ashes have not even been swept aside!"

Darya jumped up from the floor beside the hearth where she had spent the night. She looked about for a broom and fire supplies.

"Silly goose!" the woman chided, shoving Darya toward the kitchen doorway. "Everything is out in the yard. Run quickly! How will I have breakfast ready in time?"

Darya returned with a straw broom and an armful of branches and dung cakes, but swept the hearth clumsily and had no idea how to build a fire.

"No one ever trained you!" the housekeeper accused, horrified, grabbing Darya by the hair and yanking her head back. "Does the master know that he bought garbage yesterday from that dog of a slave dealer?"

Roughly, she shoved Darya away from her, and the child cowered against the wall, biting her lip and fighting back tears.

"Stop your whimpering and watch carefully now," the woman ordered, expertly stacking wood and dung in the hearth, and adding twigs and bits of cloth for kindling. Then she brushed away some ash to reveal coals still hot from the previous day's fire and blew carefully on them until the kindling caught fire. "Tomorrow morning, when I step into the kitchen, you will already have done all this for me, or you will have a beating you will not soon forget!"

The housekeeper was right: Darya did not soon forget the beating she received the next morning for mishandling the banked coals and kindling, so that the woman had to send her to a neighbor to borrow hot coals from their fire. And she did not soon forget the beating she received the following day for dropping a basket of eggs; and the day after that for spilling the leather bucket of water she had just lugged to the house from the neighborhood cistern at the end of their street.

Darya's time in the kitchen became a nightmare. The more the housekeeper yelled and beat her, the more Darya trembled and shook in her presence, and the clumsier she became. But with Monir, Darya was the complete opposite.

In the little girl's room, Darya was capable and composed. Acting well beyond her years, she kept things in order, helped the child dress, and made sure she was occupied and happy through the day. Monir doted on her, and soon, only Darya could transform Monir's pouts and frowns into smiles, and maneuver around her stubborn nature to avoid tantrums and tears.

Things came to a head after a few months when Darya turned a spit of chickens too slowly over the fire, and the special dinner the housekeeper had been preparing for the captain and his guests was burned beyond repair. She beat Darya mercilessly, accidentally pushing her into the hearth, where Darya's bare feet stepped on hot embers. Darya screamed; Monir heard the commotion, ran into the kitchen, and began crying hysterically at the sight.

"You must choose between me and that fool of a slave girl!" the housekeeper challenged her master, as he sat in the kitchen cradling his daughter in his arms to quiet her. Darya was crouched on the floor in a corner, nursing her burned feet. Never did the housekeeper imagine the master would give up her excellent cooking so that his daughter could keep her favorite slave, but the captain sent the woman packing and hired Jaleh within the week—and Darya's life was transformed.

Jaleh mothered her, plying her with food and inviting her to sleep on a mat in her bedroom instead of on the stones near the hearth in the kitchen. And Parvaneh, who arrived with her mother, treated Darya as much like a sister as a free child could treat a slave. With the encouragement of Jaleh and Parvaneh, Darya's clumsiness dissipated; she became as efficient in the kitchen as she was at caring for

Monir. And with their support, Darya learned to live with the dark, empty caverns in her mind.

"Instead of spending your time trying to pry open the doors in your head, you should be thanking all the *ahura* that they are closed," Jaleh advised her more than once. "Maybe the blessed gods of light granted you a special favor when they shut out your past. Maybe there are things behind your closed doors that the *ahura* know it is better for you not to remember."

She is probably right, Darya thought now, sweeping the hearth and skillfully building a cooking fire in the kitchen. *If my past has any connection to my awful nightmares, I am better not remembering it.* She shook her head, trying to rid it of the memory of the previous night's dream. It was one she had had many times before. There were always two pretty little girls in the dream—children whose clothing and ribbons reminded her of Monir. The children were holding hands tightly and hiding from someone or from something— something terrible—something that finally grabbed one of the girls and dragged her away.

Darya shuddered. "Blessed *ahura*, keep me safe from the terrible thing in my dreams," she whispered, parroting how she always heard Jaleh pray. But she had the unsettling feeling that the *ahura* would never listen to her, that she was not part of the circle of people under their protection. After all, had the slave dealer not said to the captain and Monir that no one knew if Darya was Persian or barbarian, or if the *ahura* were her gods too?

Three

"Birthday blessings for my darling daughter," Jaleh greeted Parvaneh two hours later in the kitchen.

The girl yawned her way into the hot, smoky room, not fully awake. She shuffled to her mother, who was sprinkling basil leaves into bean soup simmering in a pot suspended over the hearth. Jaleh hugged her with her free hand, then kissed the top of her tousled head.

"Why did you not wake me, *Ema*?" Parvaneh mumbled to her mother. "The sun is almost above the fence in the kitchen garden."

"Today you are a princess—a birthday princess." Jaleh smiled. "You are like all those beautiful young noblewomen at the palace waiting for King Xerxes to return from the war in Greece. Royalty may sleep as long as they like, and they do not need to help in the kitchen."

Parvaneh and Darya giggled, thinking of the tales they had heard about scores of noblewomen who had been ordered to gather at the palace. Each of the women was wondering if she would be chosen to replace Queen Vashti. The Queen had enraged the King—rumor had it that this was not hard to do—and she had been banished from Susa before Xerxes went off to war.

"Birthday blessings, Parvaneh," Darya called from across the kitchen where she was crouched next to a large flat stone on the floor, kneading dough for flatbread. Her words were warm, but her smile was forced. She truly wished blessings for her friend, but at the same time, she wondered what it would feel like to be hugged and kissed by a parent, or for someone to call her a princess.

"And here is some treasure for my princess," Jaleh said, producing two silver *darics* from the pocket tied to her apron.

"*Ema!*" Parvaneh exclaimed, taking the gift. "Where did you get these?"

Jaleh smiled delightedly. "For months, I have been selling my special quince jam in the market—the master allowed it—and I saved these coins for you."

"You work too hard, *Ema*, and you always give me things. There is no need."

"There *is* a need," Jaleh insisted solemnly, wiping her hands on her apron and then cupping Parvaneh's face between them. "You are *my* treasure, and I want you to know it."

"I do, *Ema*," Parvaneh murmured, hugging her.

Darya lowered her eyes and concentrated on kneading the bread dough, feeling as though she were intruding on something private. But suddenly she became aware that Jaleh was standing above her, and amazingly, she was holding out another silver *daric*.

"This is for you, Darya," Jaleh said kindly. "We have never had any way of knowing when to give you birthday blessings, so I have decided to do it today, on the same day as Parvaneh. Today, you are both twelve years old."

Darya was at a loss for words. She wanted to tell Jaleh how much the gift meant to her—how much Jaleh and Parvaneh meant to her—but she did not know how. Instead she stammered, "Th-Thank you, madam—but what will I do with it?"

Jaleh bent down and placed her hand gently on Darya's shoulder. "You will put it in a safe place, girl, and keep it. And you will add to it whenever you can, until you have enough to buy your freedom."

Freedom? Darya echoed in her mind. She had never thought of that possibility. She was a slave and had never imagined she might someday be something else. "Is that something I could really do—someday?" she asked hesitantly.

Jaleh squeezed her shoulder. "It is, girl. Always remember that. And I will help you if I can. Now put the coin out of sight and—"

"Yes, put it out of sight before someone makes it disappear," came a gravelly male voice from the doorway that led into the kitchen courtyard.

Jaleh spun around to face a man who was lounging against the door jamb. His blue tunic and white trousers were as spotless as the clothes the army captain always wore, his forehead was circled with a finely coiled headband, and his hair and beard were neatly trimmed and curled. But while the captain's appearance inspired comfort and reassurance, this man made Darya shudder whenever she saw him. Perhaps it was the way he held his head back and looked down at people with squinting eyes and a smirk on his lips. She noticed that Parvaneh seemed uneasy, too. Jaleh, on the other hand, was always ready to do battle with him.

"You again, Behrooz!" she fumed. "You were here not two months ago. What do you want from me now?"

"What do I want?" he mused calmly. "For a start, perhaps some of that quince jam you are so proud of, and then we will talk of other things."

Jaleh blew out a breath and glanced quickly at the two girls. "Into the yard with you," she ordered Behrooz, striding toward the man and shooing him out the door. "We will talk outside."

"As you wish, my dear Jaleh," Behrooz responded, bowing to her slightly with exaggerated politeness. "But one day it will be time to talk in front of this pampered daughter of yours and this very hard-working slave girl. They are both growing up, and one day we will—"

"Out!" Jaleh shouted, pushing him into the yard. "It is enough that you keep appearing like a snake slithering out from under a rock. I do not need to hear your threats. May the *daeva* take you!"

Behrooz laughed maliciously. "If the *daeva* take me, they will surely want you to come along, dear Jaleh, because—"

Jaleh slammed the door shut behind her, and Darya and Parvaneh could hear no more. "Does she ever talk to you about him?" Darya asked her friend worriedly. The way

Behrooz had said "pampered daughter" and "slave girl" had made her shiver.

Parvaneh shook her head. "I have asked her many times, but she says nothing. You can see that she hates him, yet she always speaks to him and never calls Nasim to make him leave."

Darya pictured Nasim, the old slave who moved stiffly, gardening and caring for the household's goats and chickens, and imagined him standing up to powerful Behrooz. "I do not think Nasim could force Master Behrooz to do anything he did not want to do," she said thoughtfully. "I wish the captain were at home."

"It seems he has been away forever," Parvaneh replied. "And anyway, Master Behrooz never comes by when the captain is at home. Have you not noticed that?" She craned her neck to see if she could glimpse her mother and Behrooz out the kitchen window. Then she said, "How long has the captain been gone? Eight moons?"

"Longer," Darya said. "Almost a year. He was summoned to the war in Greece right after the summer, and now it is summer again. Monir misses him terribly."

Darya sighed, covered the flatbread with a cloth, and left it to rise so it would be ready for Jaleh to bake later. The housekeeper would slap the thin loaves against the hot walls of the beehive oven in the yard, where they would stick until they were baked. Meanwhile, Darya filled a wooden tray with goat cheese that she had helped Jaleh make the previous week, and dates from a tree in the garden. She added some of yesterday's flatbread, a small bowl of seasoned sesame oil to dip it in, and a cup of fresh goat milk. For good measure, she laid on the tray a large orange flower from the hibiscus bush outside the kitchen doorway.

"Monir is probably awake by now," she said, lifting the tray and walking toward the second kitchen door that led into the rest of the house. Then she stopped. "It will be all right," she reassured Parvaneh, glancing over her shoulder toward the closed door of the courtyard. "Your *Ema* can handle Master Behrooz."

Parvaneh smiled wanly and nodded, but neither girl was entirely certain Jaleh would always be able to handle the man. "I had better get dressed," Parvaneh said. "After all, it is my birthday and I have two silver coins to spend on sweets and pretty things."

And I have a silver coin too, Darya thought in wonder, walking toward Monir's room. *Perhaps to buy my freedom.*

Four

Darya spent the rest of the morning with Monir. After pouring water from a pitcher into a gaily painted earthenware bowl, Darya helped her young mistress wash. Then she helped her dress in one of the many colorful outfits her father ordered from dressmakers, with knee-length tunics, pantaloons, and embroidered vests. She brushed the girl's dark hair until it glistened like liquid ebony, and decorated it with ribbons—lavender and pink were her favorites. Darya held up a bronze mirror for Monir to admire herself, then replaced it on the table, but not before catching an unexpected glimpse of her own image.

It always startled her to see herself. She was accustomed to looking at Monir, bright and brushed, wearing fine linen or silk; or at Parvaneh, neatly turned out in simple woolen dresses, but invariably sporting bright ribbons or shiny clips that Jaleh had bought for her. She was never prepared for her own appearance: dark hair caught severely behind her head to keep it out of the food and the cooking fire; oval face often smudged from the hearth; a coarse, colorless, shapeless tunic that faded into the background; and, of course, the iron collar around her neck.

The captain had never considered using the collar for anything, and had even remarked once or twice that he should take Darya to a blacksmith to have it removed, especially when it began chafing her neck as she grew, but he never had. And so the collar remained, forever reminding Darya of who she was. Parvaneh once told her she was pretty, but Darya could not imagine how her friend could say that about the image she had just seen in the mirror.

While Monir ate her breakfast in the small courtyard garden enclosed in the center of the house, then skipped among the flower beds, Darya cleaned and aired the girl's room, emptying the night soil from her chamber pot into the covered pit near the animal stalls in the far corner of the kitchen courtyard.

Cleaning the room took longer than necessary because of all the interruptions from Monir, who often called Darya into the courtyard to examine a spider web or to help catch a butterfly. This was something Darya particularly liked about her young mistress: the wonder and pleasure she derived from the world around her. And these types of interruptions were certainly preferable to the bouts of crying when Monir thought of her father fighting in a war in a distant land. They were also preferable to dealing with Monir's pouts and stubbornness when it was time for her to review the lessons her tutor had left for her.

For lunch, Jaleh and Parvaneh brought bowls of bean soup and fresh flatbread into the courtyard, and the four of them picnicked together under an awning that shielded them from the hot sun. Jaleh was subdued, as she usually was after a visit from Behrooz. But Parvaneh bubbled over about her morning visit to the market with her mother. She wore an embroidered shawl, as pretty as one of Monir's, that she had purchased with one of her birthday coins. And she shared some of the candied orange peels she had also bought.

Darya complimented her friend's purchases while she stealthily fingered her own silver coin, which was safely hidden in a tuck she had sewn in her tunic. Once again, she thought of the idea of buying freedom and wondered what her life would be like if she were not a slave. Where would she live? How would she eat? Who would protect her if someone like Master Behrooz wanted to harm her? Darya looked around the flowering courtyard, with its central fountain of collected rainwater cooling the heated air, and was grateful once again that the captain had bought her in the slave market six years ago. Then she looked at Jaleh and Parvaneh. If she were free, would she lose her friends? Would she be left to deal with her nightmares alone?

It was a relief to Darya when Monir's tutor arrived, forcing her to set her troubling thoughts aside and concentrate on his lessons. This was young Master Saeed's first position, and he took his job very seriously. The captain had attempted to hire a more experienced teacher, but could not find one who was willing to teach a girl the types of things the captain wanted his daughter to learn.

"Would you try to teach a chicken to give milk?" one of the tutors had taunted the captain when he came to the house for an interview.

Master Saeed, on the other hand, in his frayed tunic and worn sandals, was so desperate for a job that he would have been willing to try to teach the goats to dance if the captain were willing to pay him for it. As usual, when the tutor entered Monir's room, he was depending upon Darya to learn everything he taught so that she could guide and encourage Monir in his absence. Monir was usually much more interested in an ant crawling along the edge of a floor tile, or a bird perching on her windowsill, than she was in learning to read or to cipher. But today the girl was fully attentive. A letter had arrived from the captain, and reading it would be the subject of Master Saeed's lesson.

"Sit beside me, Mistress Monir," the tutor said, as he unrolled the papyrus scroll on a low polished wooden table in Monir's room. "And you, Darya, over here," he added, indicating a thick floor cushion on his other side. "Now, before we begin, let us see what you remember from your father's other letters. Where is your father fighting, Mistress Monir?"

"My *Aba* is in Greece, Master Saeed," Monir replied with assurance.

"And where is Greece?"

"It is to the west, past the end of the long Royal Road that begins here in Susa and goes through Anatolia to Sardis. Then across the Hellespont, across ... across...."

Monir stopped, at a loss, and the tutor turned toward Darya.

"Across Thrace and Macedonia," Darya filled in.

"You are doing well, Mistress Monir," Saeed encouraged. "Now tell me *why* your father is fighting there."

Monir thought for a moment. "Because the people there were helping bad Greeks," she said, trying to remember. "The bad people were living in...." She looked toward Darya for help. "I can never think of the names!" she complained.

"Ionia," Darya prompted her.

"Yes, Ionia. Ungrateful people—who fought against our great King Darius even though he allowed them to live how they wanted. And they burned one of our cities. They burned—"

"Sardis," said Darya.

"Oh, yes, of course—Sardis," repeated Monir. "So later our great King Xerxes went to *their* country and won a big fight in their mountains at a place called ... called...."

Darya racked her brain for the name of the mountain pass. "Th ... Th...." she attempted.

Saeed laughed. "Not even Darya remembers this one. It is Thermopylae," he told the girls.

Darya mouthed the word silently, trying to memorize it.

"And then King Xerxes burned one of their cities," continued Monir. "He burned—"

"Athens," Darya said.

"You remembered many things, Mistress Monir," Saeed said, pleased. "Soon after the burning of Athens is when your father was summoned to Greece. Do you remember why?"

Monir was silent and Saeed began to turn toward Darya for an answer, but Monir said softly, "I know why my *Aba* went to Greece, Master Saeed. He told me."

"What did he tell you?" asked Saeed gently.

Monir's eyes grew wide. "He said that there was a very big fight in the sea, but I do not remember the name of the place again."

"Salamis," Darya said quietly.

Monir nodded and continued in the same small voice, "My *Aba* said many good Persian soldiers were killed by the Greeks at Salamis." Her face and voice brightened for a moment as she added, "But he also told me about the Queen of Caria—her name is Artimesia, I think—he wanted me to know that even though she is a woman, she is a great fighter. She commanded some of the ships for the Persians and King Xerxes praised her." Monir's face darkened again, as she continued. "But most of the other Persian ships were destroyed, and so King Xerxes needed more soldiers to come fight with him … and my *Aba* had to go." She shivered and looked as though she might cry.

The three of them sat silently for a few moments until Saeed said kindly, "Mistress Monir, your father has told you things, and I have taught you things, that girls— especially young girls your age—do not usually hear about. He treats you—and he wants me to treat you—like someone much older, and maybe even like a boy. But that is because he believes you can be like Queen Artimesia, strong enough and smart enough to know these things. Do you understand?"

Monir nodded. She took a deep breath, wiped her eyes with the back of her hand, and sat up straight. "May we read my *Aba*'s letter now?"

Darya looked at her young mistress with admiration, amazed that the girl was able to control her fears for her father away at war.

The tutor smoothed the papyrus and asked Monir to begin to read. She leaned forward and studied the scroll, trying to decipher the lettering. Darya, too, leaned forward, knowing she would be called upon to help. She was relieved to see that the letter had been written in Aramaic, which she could read easily by now. Occasionally, the captain wrote his letters in the more formal Persian, making Darya struggle through the many wedge shapes almost as much as Monir did.

"*My darling daughter,*" Monir began hesitantly, concentrating carefully on each word.

"*It is so….*" Monir's voice trailed off.

"Darya?" Saeed prompted.

"*So long,*" Darya filled in.

"*It is so long since I last saw you,*" Monir went on. "*Eight moons.*" She looked up. "Eight moons? He has been away almost eleven moons. I know, because I make a mark for each moon on the date tree in the courtyard."

"Your father is far away," Saeed explained, "with the army in a foreign land. Our *angarium*—our post service—is the best in the world, but we do not know how long it took for this scroll to reach Persian soil."

Monir turned back to the papyrus. "*Eight moons*," she repeated. "*You must be all grown up by now.*" She giggled. "Oh, *Aba*," she said, as though her father were there in the room. "I am still only ten years old."

She leaned over the papyrus again, and with Darya helping and Saeed supplying the words neither of the girls could decipher, she read the letter through to the end.

"*The war drags on*," the captain had written.

It keeps me here in these foreign mountains, far away from the lowlands of my beloved city of Susa. The Greeks build grand temples to their gods instead of worshiping them beneath the open heavens, as we do around the Sacred Fire of Ahura Mazda. They create fine marble statues and glorious monuments, but nothing here is as lovely to me as the soft air in our own courtyard, and the colorful patterns in our carpets and gardens.

The people here also have strange ideas. My dear Monir, I now begin to understand how they dared revolt against our great King Darius in Ionia, even though he gave them so much freedom to live as they wished. The cities in Greece are not united under one great king, as we are—one good king who leads their army and protects them and is concerned for their well-being. They constantly squabble with each other and fight to see which one will rule the others.

And some of the cities, like Athens, even believe in what they call "democracy," a foolish notion that the people should decide on their own laws and choose their own rulers. Royalty and breeding mean nothing to them. Any free-born man among them can rise to become their leader—even though only some are worthy and others are not—and then he can be dragged down again, if the common people become displeased with him.

I dream of this war ending quickly, and marching home victorious to my own great country. Until then, my Monir, be sure to attend to your studies, and heed Madame Jaleh and Master Saeed. Do not forget you are the mistress of the household and must always follow the teachings of our great prophet Zoroaster to be truthful and good. He would especially want you to be kind to Parvaneh, Nasim, and Darya.

Most of all, my darling daughter, always remember that there is nothing in this life as dear to me as you.

Your loving Aba

Silence filled the room when Monir finished reading. Darya knew that she was crying quietly. For Darya's part, she kept rereading the last sentence. Had she ever had a father or a mother who felt that way about her? Who were they? Were they still alive? Were they slaves, as she was? Or had they been killed in a war somewhere, leaving Darya to be taken prisoner and carried off in a slave caravan?

Saeed cleared his throat. "Your reading has truly improved, Mistress Monir," he complimented her. "For tomorrow, practice reading this letter with Darya so that you will be able to decipher it entirely by yourself." He struggled up from his low seat, looking like a long-necked heron as he arched his back and stretched his tall, thin frame. "It is time for me to go, and it is time for you to take your afternoon rest."

Five

After Darya helped Monir undress and settled her in her soft featherbed, she returned to the kitchen where Jaleh was beginning preparations for supper. The housekeeper still seemed to have a dark cloud hovering above her, but Parvaneh was in high spirits. Since her mother refused to let her work on her birthday, she was flitting about the kitchen with her arms spread out, watching her gauzy shawl ripple in the breeze she was creating.

"You look like a butterfly," Darya said, smiling at her friend. She squatted on the floor to scrape the scales off the fish Jaleh had purchased that morning.

"I *am* a butterfly," Parvaneh sang. "Did you know that? *Parvaneh* means 'butterfly' in Persian. Is that not so, *Ema*?"

Jaleh looked up from the vegetable stew she was preparing and made a visible effort to join in her daughter's happy mood. "Yes, my darling. I chose that name for you."

"Why?" Parvaneh asked, alighting on a stool near the hearth where her mother was working. "Did you know what it meant?"

"Of course I knew," Jaleh assured her. "When you were growing inside me, I went to pray at the fire-altar of *Ahura Mazda*, and one of the old *magi* tending the fire cautioned me to name you carefully when you were born. He said that a person's name is important, that it can have an influence on a person's life. And I wanted you to have a life like a butterfly—colorful and happy and free and…."

Her voice trailed off and Parvaneh jumped up to begin flitting about the room again. "Thank you for my name, *Ema*," she called gaily. Then she stopped abruptly and asked her mother, "Did your parents do the same for you—choose a name that would be good for your life?"

"May the *ahura* forgive me, but I do not like my name," Jaleh said flatly. "It means 'rain.'"

"But rain is good," Parvaneh pointed out. "It brings life."

"Not always," Jaleh shot back. "On days like today I feel like I am being rained on, like I am in a storm."

"Because of Master Behrooz," Parvaneh said knowingly. "I wonder what *his* name means."

"It means 'lucky,'" Jaleh told her bitterly. "Why would the *ahura* want someone like him to be lucky?"

"Who is he, Madame?" Darya asked cautiously. "Why does he come here?"

Jaleh flapped her hand at Darya as though shooing flies off the food. "He is nothing. Nothing! And I do not want you or Parvaneh to worry about him or even think about him."

Parvaneh sank onto a stool and Darya lowered her head toward the fish she was cleaning. "What about Darya's name?" asked Parvaneh, trying to lighten the mood again. "Is her name also Persian? And do you know what it means?"

"How would I know about Darya's name?" Jaleh demanded irritably. But then she took a deep breath and muttered more calmly, "I think … yes … it is Persian." She turned her attention toward the stew again and said impatiently, "I think it means 'someone who protects,' someone who saves other people."

"That is a good name for you," Parvaneh said, looking down at Darya, "because you always take good care of Monir."

"A protector," Darya said thoughtfully. "I wonder if my parents knew what the name meant when they gave it to me."

"If they were Persian they would have known," Jaleh commented, still focusing on the stew.

With the back of her hand, Darya brushed away some fish scales that her knife had flicked onto her forehead. But she stopped suddenly, trying to sort out a memory that had jumped into her mind. It was of that day in the slave market so long ago, the day she had first seen Monir and the captain. Monir had come close to her and asked her name, and she remembered now that it was not she who had responded. It was the slave dealer who said, "She is called Darya."

"Perhaps it was not even my parents who named me," Darya said now, still trying to make sense of the memory. "Perhaps it was the slave dealer."

"Why would he call you a protector?" Parvaneh asked.

Darya shrugged. "He might not even have known what the name meant. He spoke Aramaic. Maybe he just wanted a name that sounded Persian."

"It makes no difference who named you," Jaleh said, with a tinge of sharpness in her voice. "What is important is that Darya is your name now, and you must live up to it. That is what the *ahura* want from you."

Darya was taken aback. Jaleh had never spoken harshly to her before. She sensed that she should be silent, but too many questions were crowding her mind. Hesitantly, she asked, "How can I know what the *ahura* want from me? Perhaps I am not even Persian." She thought for a minute and added, "The slave dealer told the captain that he did not know—"

"Stop this silliness," Jaleh burst out. "Wherever you came from, the *ahura* put you with that slave dealer for a reason, and they put you here for a reason, just like Parvaneh and I are here for a reason. They sent the captain to war, and they brought Behrooz here this morning—all for a reason. And we must all accept it. Now enough!"

Darya and Parvaneh glanced at each other with wide, frightened eyes. Neither of them dared speak again. Darya turned back to preparing the fish, while Parvaneh rose silently and slipped quietly out of the kitchen, her butterfly shawl wrapped around her like protective wings.

∞

Darya had trouble sleeping that night. For the first time, being on the floor of Jaleh's room was not a comfort to her, and she thought she might even feel better alone near the hearth in the kitchen. Jaleh's outburst had hung over her and Parvaneh all evening, while Darya reviewed the captain's letter with Monir and helped her embroider a section of a new wall-hanging that would be a surprise for the captain when he returned. As the summer dusk began to gather, Darya served Monir the fish and vegetables for supper, then, under Nasim's watchful eye, the three girls took a walk along their quiet street of walled villas until it was time for Monir to go to bed.

We are all here for a reason and we must all accept it. Jaleh's words and the way she had said them rumbled through Darya's mind like grindstones endlessly turning. *Is there a reason that I am a slave?* she asked herself, examining the thought from all angles as she lay on her mat. *Is there a reason that I am in this house and not somewhere else?* She thought back to the slave market again. *If the slave dealer had packed up his awning a few minutes earlier, Monir and her father would never have seen me. They would never have bought me.* Darya shuddered. Everything would have been different.

And is there a reason that my past hides behind a blank wall? she wondered for the thousandth time. Was Jaleh right? Were the *ahura* protecting her by keeping her past hidden? If that were so, then the *ahura* cared about her. She was part of their circle—a Persian girl with a good Persian name: Darya, the protector. But who was she supposed to protect? She did not really think of herself as Monir's protector, in spite of what Parvaneh had said. She was Monir's slave.

Darya finally fell into a fitful sleep, troubled by her recurrent dream of the pretty little girls hiding in the garden. This time, one of the girls was Monir, and Darya was there to protect her from something terrible lurking nearby. But the garden was so dark. It was impossible for Darya to locate the danger. She heard Monir scream and tried to help her, but she could not find her. The little girl had been swallowed up by the blackness.

Darya woke up in a sweat and looked toward the unshuttered window. Dawn was not yet breaking, but she could not lie on her mat any longer. She crept out of the room and made her way through the dark house to the kitchen, where she curled up, exhausted, in front of the hearth. And that was where Jaleh shook her awake in the morning.

"Are you all right, Darya? You have never slept late like this. The fire is not lit."

Darya jumped up, feeling nauseous and dizzy. She stumbled toward the courtyard for logs, dung, and kindling, and laid a clumsy fire in the hearth. Slowly her head cleared—but not the memory of her terrible dream. It draped itself heavily about her all day, wrapping her in foreboding until late afternoon, during Monir's nap, when Nasim burst into the kitchen.

"It is over!" the old slave cried. "The servants next door heard it in the market. It is over!"

"What is over, old man?" Jaleh demanded. "What are you jabbering about?"

"The war. Post riders have come." Nasim slowly lowered his stiff body onto a stone ledge near the hearth. "There was a terrible battle at a place called Plataea. Many were killed on both sides, and King Xerxes said it was enough. We had punished the Greeks enough, and it was time to come home."

"Praise *Ahura Mazda*," Jaleh murmured. "Darya, quick, bring Nasim some water. And wake up Monir. Tell her the captain will be coming home!"

Six

Years later, whenever Darya thought back to this day and the ones that followed, what she saw over and over was Monir's face. First, when she heard that her father was returning, a face so luminous that her own private sun could have been shining out from inside her. And then, two days later, when new post riders arrived in Susa with long lists of the soldiers who would never come home from Greece, a face so terrifyingly tortured it looked like it belonged in the world of the *daeva*. The captain was on the lists.

Darya did not know if she herself was physically ill or simply battered down by the awful news, but from the time of Jaleh's outburst in the kitchen, her mind had been clouded and her head heavy. Her limbs seemed sluggish, as though she were wading through filthy muck to do her chores. And the more she felt the need to be alert and wary of the goings-on around her, the less capable she felt.

Monir's uncle and aunt arrived from the chief capital city of Persepolis a week after they received the devastating news. Darya served them cold tea and oranges that had been chilled in the cellar, which kept cool because it was located right next to a *kariz*, an underground canal that

supplied water to the city. The relatives sat with Jaleh and
Monir in the courtyard garden, discussing the girl's future.

"You will come live with us," the captain's older brother
said kindly to his niece. He was stouter than the captain
had been, and not as tall. "You do not know us well, but
we are your only family. Do you remember that we have
three children? Your cousins—a girl and boy who are
older than you, and another boy who is your age. We live
in a villa much like this one, with a courtyard in the center.
You will feel at home."

Monir sat on a stone bench close to Jaleh, whose arm
was around her shoulders protectively. "We must leave
Susa?" Monir asked with a catch in her voice.

"You have nobody here," her uncle explained. "We will
sell this house and put some of the money away for your
dowry."

"But Jaleh is here," Monir protested softly. "And
Parvaneh, and Darya and Nasim. And my tutor, Master
Saeed, comes almost every day."

"They are not your family, dear," Monir's aunt said,
smoothing the fine silk of her green print dress across
her lap. She was an exceedingly bony woman who sat very
straight and tall, and looked every inch like a resident of
the kingdom's grand capital city. "They are all servants
and slaves."

Monir glanced up at Jaleh beside her. "Will you and
Parvaneh come with me if I must go to Persepolis?"

Jaleh squeezed her shoulders. "I am glad to come, Mistress Monir. But it is up to your aunt and uncle."

Monir's uncle cleared his throat. "I am afraid that will not be possible. I am only a merchant. Our house is not large. And we already have a housekeeper and cook. But out of respect for my brother's memory, I will help you find another position."

Monir began to cry quietly and snuggled closer to Jaleh, as though that would be able to keep them together. "Madame Jaleh takes care of me," she said plaintively.

"Now, child," Monir's aunt said with a touch of irritation in her voice. "Your uncle and I will take care of you. You will not be alone."

"It will be all right, sweet child," Jaleh comforted her, stroking her hair. "You will be with your family. And Darya will be there." But as she spoke the words, Jaleh looked up with a stricken expression on her face. "She *will* be there. Is that not so? Monir will be able to keep her own slave."

The uncle began to nod hesitantly, but his wife said quickly, "My husband just told you that our house is not large. We have all the servants and slaves that we can afford. The child will have all of her needs taken care of by the slaves already under our roof."

Monir's expression turned to one of panic, and Darya stood frozen near the table of drinks and fruit. It had never occurred to her that she might be separated from Monir. What did that mean? What did these relatives have in mind for her?

"The house will be put up for sale along with everything that belongs to it: the furniture, the animals, and the slaves," Monir's uncle said uncomfortably. Darya's heart began pounding and a wave of dizziness swept over her. She placed one hand on the table to steady herself, and with the other she pulled at the slave collar that suddenly felt as though it were choking her. "We must raise the funds to add another child to our household and to provide a dowry for her when she is grown. This is what my brother would have wanted." The uncle had not looked at Monir or met Jaleh's eyes as he spoke.

"No!" Monir cried, her stubborn nature rising through her grief. "*Aba* wanted me to have Darya. He took me to the slave market to find her when I was four years old and he bought her for me." She laid her head on Jaleh's lap and sobbed into her apron.

"You are *ten* years old now, Monir," her aunt said sternly. "Your father would not want you to be making such a scene. You do not need your own slave anymore."

"She takes care of my things," Monir insisted desperately, her voice muffled in Jaleh's lap. "And she practices my lessons with me. She helps me read the words I do not know."

Monir's aunt and uncle stared at her, dumbfounded, and then her aunt gave a short, barking laugh. "You are learning to read?" she asked, staring at her niece as though the girl had sprouted a second head. "And your slave helps you?"

"Yes," Monir said, sitting up hopefully. "My *Aba* wanted to be sure I could run this household or a business if I ever needed to—that I would not be cheated. But I have trouble learning the shapes and signs, and Darya helps me. I need her to come to Persepolis with me."

"You do not!" her aunt replied emphatically, no longer laughing. "Because we will not permit any such foolishness in our house. Learning to read! Running a business! The very idea! No one in our household has wasted time with reading, except for your uncle, who is a merchant. And our daughter has never had a tutor for anything. She has been taught embroidery and painting and how to manage a household—all the things a respectable young woman should learn. Without reading! She will certainly not be out mixing with men in the business world, even though our King has seen fit to allow it!" The woman rose and turned toward her husband. "My dear, I have had enough of this nonsense. The child is only ten years old. We must make the proper decisions for her future." She turned toward Darya. "You are Monir's slave. Is that correct?"

"Yes, madam," Darya said, her mouth dry.

"Go to her room now and begin packing her things. We must leave for home at first light tomorrow morning, and everything must be ready."

Darya's legs felt like soft clay. She did not think she could take a step. She looked at Monir, sobbing again on Jaleh's lap, and at the aunt's angry face. Then she turned to the uncle, who seemed disturbed by how upset Monir was. "Sir, please," she begged. "Mistress Monir is so … I would eat very little … I can sleep outside … Please…."

Whatever else she might have said was cut off by the resounding slap she received from Monir's aunt, who had stepped around the table.

"Out!" she yelled at Darya. "What sort of household did your brother run?" she demanded of her husband. "Slaves that argue ... Girls learning to read and run businesses...."

"Calm yourself, my dear," he said soothingly to his wife. He looked very much like his brother now, as he rose and moved toward Monir, who was staring horrified at her aunt. "Come, child," he said gently, blocking her view of the red welts that were rising on Darya's cheek. "Let us take a stroll outside while Darya packs your things."

Monir hung back, but Jaleh pushed her toward her uncle. "Go, child," she whispered. "It will be all right."

Then the housekeeper stood up and walked to the table, stepping purposefully between the aunt and Darya, who was rubbing her face in stunned silence. Without even glancing at the woman, Jaleh said in a level voice meant to help Darya regain her composure, "Parvaneh will help you do the packing, girl. Come with me now to the storage room to find a trunk."

Seven

The house echoed emptily after Monir and her relatives left the next morning for the five-day journey to Persepolis. Besides their own carriage, they had hired a wagon for Monir's wicker trunk and for the straw baskets and cloth bags of possessions they wanted from the house. Darya kept picturing them leaving, growing smaller as they traveled down the road, and her goodbyes to Monir reverberated in her head.

"Will I ever see you again?" Monir had moaned, clinging to Darya at the gate of the villa in spite of her aunt's disapproval at her showing such affection for a slave.

"It is something we can pray for, Mistress Monir. Perhaps the *ahura* will make it happen," Darya had murmured, not knowing how else to comfort the girl. Then a thought came to her. "Mistress, perhaps we can write letters to each other, just like your father wrote to you from Greece."

Monir swallowed a sob and looked up. "May I do that?" she asked her relatives. "I am sure my father would have wanted it."

Her aunt pursed her lips but her uncle said quickly, "Certainly. We will supply you with papyrus and ink." He pulled a leather money pouch from a fold in his tunic and shook a few small coins into his palm. "Here, Madame Jaleh," he said, pressing the coins into the housekeeper's hand. "This is for you to purchase what Darya needs to write to her mistress."

Monir was able to gain enough control of herself after that to let go of Darya and climb into the carriage. Jaleh, Parvaneh, Darya, and Nasim managed to keep smiles on their faces and wave to her as she rode off. But now they sat together on small stools around the low kitchen table as though in mourning, staring at nothing. Jaleh had set out flatbread and cheese, even her special quince jam—she had said there was no longer any reason to save it—but no one ate.

"What will become of us, Madame Jaleh?" Nasim asked, looking as though he had shrunk since yesterday.

"We must set the house in order," Jaleh said listlessly. "Clean everything so it will attract buyers. The family hired an agent who will come later today to see what is here and to set prices."

"What will we do when the house is sold, *Ema*?" Parvaneh asked.

"The agent will help us find a new place," Jaleh assured her. "That is what Monir's uncle promised. People always need cooks and housekeepers."

"Will we bring Darya and Nasim to the new place?" Parvaneh asked hesitantly, exchanging worried glances with her friend.

Jaleh looked down at the table. She took a piece of bread and began tearing small pieces from it and rolling them nervously between her fingers. "I cannot promise that," she said in a flat voice. "Perhaps our new employer will want two slaves as well as us, but perhaps not. It will be in the hands of the agent." She looked at her daughter and Darya, who now sat slumped with hopeless expressions on their faces. "We can wait to see who buys Darya and Nasim, and then we can ask the agent to try to help us be hired there," she suggested, in an attempt to cheer them.

"Who will want to buy a stiff old man?" Nasim asked plaintively. "I will end my days in the poorhouse." He shook his head. "I would be better off dead, like the captain."

"Hush," Jaleh said, patting his shoulder. "The *ahura* will take care of you."

Nasim grunted. "In times such as these, the *ahura* do not concern themselves with old slaves—not with all the dead and wounded from the war. The slaves next door told me that soldiers are already starting to return. And they are not saying the same thing as the King's post riders of the *angarium*."

"What do you mean?" Jaleh asked.

"'We have punished the Greeks enough.' That is what the riders told everyone, do you remember? 'King Xerxes said it is time to go home.'" Nasim laughed shortly, showing the dark gaps in his mouth where teeth had rotted away.

"What are the soldiers saying, Nasim?" Parvaneh prompted him.

"That the Greeks won the war. They killed our General Mardonius and pushed our army out of their country. That is why there are so many dead and wounded."

"Silly old man!" Jaleh exclaimed. "King Xerxes gathered the largest and strongest army the world ever saw to fight the Greeks! No enemy could survive the arrows of our archers and the lances of our cavalry. The Empire stretches from India to Nubia! Who are the Greeks to be able to push us out?"

"I am telling you what the soldiers are saying. That is all I know," Nasim insisted.

"If it is true, how will the King act when he returns?" Jaleh wondered. "Will he admit to a defeat?"

"Now it is you who are the silly old woman!" Nasim cried. "I am only an old slave, but I have seen and heard much in my sixty years in this world. I could tell you stories of how kings act, how they hide things … I could tell you stories…." His voice trailed off and his watery eyes seemed to be looking at something in the far distance.

"Then tell us," Jaleh demanded, bristling that he had called her a silly old woman. "Share your great wisdom!"

Nasim focused his gaze on her and rubbed the stubble on his sharp chin. "If you truly want to know. I grew up hearing the legends about our great King Cyrus, who put this Empire together when he conquered the Medes in the north. Now *there* was a leader, Madame Jaleh," he said, slapping the table for emphasis. "*There* was a leader who did not need to cover up defeat."

"Who was king when you were a boy?" Parvaneh asked.

"It was the son of King Cyrus, Cambyses—he was weak and cruel, not a worthy son for such a king," Nasim said.

"Cambyses was one who needed to hide things. He added Egypt to the Empire, but he was hated, and one of the priests stole his throne from him."

"Truly?" Parvaneh asked, enthralled. "What did the King do?"

Nasim grunted. "He rushed home from Egypt to try to take it back, but something happened along the way—something that was covered up." Nasim clucked his tongue. "He was killed by a sword, but people were never told who was holding it—whether his enemies killed him, or whether he killed himself."

"Why would a king kill himself?" Darya asked, as fascinated as Parvaneh.

"He could have been forced to by his enemies," Jaleh suggested, and Nasim nodded vigorously. Encouraged, Jaleh continued, "Or he could have realized he did not have enough power to take back his throne and decided this was the better way to die, instead of being exiled or tortured or murdered."

"How long did the priest rule?" Parvaneh asked.

"Not even a year," Nasim retorted. "Our great King Darius, a far-off cousin of King Cambyses, took control of the army and that was the end of him."

"How do you know all this, Nasim?" Parvaneh asked with admiration.

The old slave smiled and held up his work-calloused hands. "I use these to take care of the gardens and the animals," he said. "But I use these"—he pointed to his eyes and ears—"to find out what is happening around me." He cackled. "I was not always a slave, you know. I was once a free man who could think and act for myself."

They all stared at him. "Why did you never tell us?" Jaleh asked, astonished.

Nasim hunched his shoulders and hung his head. "It is not something to be proud of," he muttered. "I was a merchant, like Monir's uncle. But I was cheated and lost everything. I was sold into debt slavery and could never buy my way out." He shook his head. "Now I am too old."

Darya looked at the old man more closely than she ever had before—at his soiled and ragged clothes, the dirt ingrained in the skin of his hands, his leathery face—and wondered what he had been like before he became a slave. It had never occurred to her that someone like Nasim might have a mind as sharp as Master Saeed's, but no one had ever before cared to hear what he had to say.

"King Darius was another one who did not need to hide things from the people. Is that not so, Nasim?" Jaleh asked, trying to turn the old man's attention away from his troubled thoughts. "He was King until just a few years ago."

Nasim took a deep breath and nodded emphatically. "For thirty-six years he put down rebellions and organized the Empire and made it strong. He is the one who started building Persepolis and laid the roads and made the coins."

"That must be why they are called *darics*!" Parvaneh exclaimed.

Jaleh nodded. "And King Darius dug the *qanats*, the long tunnels, to bring water from the mountains to the farmers, and the *kariz* to bring water to the cisterns in the city streets. And he set up stations along the Royal Road so that the post riders of the *angarium* could pass along his messages and the mail to fresh riders and horses. That is how they can deliver things as quickly as they do."

"Yet now we are ruled by King Xerxes," Nasim said, "who is not the kind of king his father was."

"But he has done great things," Darya insisted. "The captain wrote to Mistress Monir that he built fabulous floating bridges across the Hellespont for the soldiers to cross—bridges resting on rows of boats. And he dug a canal for the warships...."

Nasim nodded. "He has done great things, Darya, but he is also known for his drinking and his pride and his temper—especially his temper!—which is why we do not have a queen now in Susa. He drank too much and banished Queen Vashti in a rage. And now he has lost a war. What does a king like that do when he loses a war?" The old slave looked around the table, fully enjoying this unusual experience of being the center of attention. "He comes home and tries to make people forget that it ever happened!"

"How will he do that?" Parvaneh asked him, still captivated.

Nasim shrugged his shoulders, but Jaleh exclaimed, "Perhaps by having a royal wedding!"

The Seventh Handmaiden

"All those women are waiting for him in the palace," Parvaneh remembered. "He needs to replace the Queen. The palace will be a very busy place when the King returns."

They all laughed, the tension broken, and began enjoying the food before them.

Eight

But Darya realized that nothing had been resolved for her or Nasim. She started to worry again about where they would be sold. She dreaded being taken away by strangers, and she pictured herself in the slave market again, being prodded and examined. Would she be as lucky this time as she had been with the captain and Monir? And would the agent want to be bothered about finding a place where they could all be together? Darya felt that she had to find a way to stay with Jaleh and Parvaneh or she would not survive. And then an idea came to her that made her breathe in sharply. The others stopped eating and looked at her.

"What is it, girl?" Jaleh asked.

"The palace," she said, trying to put her thoughts into words. The others kept looking at her, confused. "The palace," she repeated. "It will be very busy."

"Yes," Jaleh agreed. "That is what Parvaneh said."

"They will need many servants," Darya continued. "All of those women. And now the King returning. There will be dinners and parties. Perhaps they will want all of us—together."

Jaleh considered. "You might have something there," she murmured. "They would want experienced people, and we are all experienced. And people with good reputations, which we have—the servants of a captain in the King's army. People who are worthy—the servants of a soldier who died for the King."

"And would they not want young girls in the women's quarters, *Ema*?" Parvaneh asked.

"I would think so," Jaleh responded. "They have guards to protect the women, but they need girls to serve them."

"They will also need many cooks," Darya put in. "And more people in the stables once the King returns with all of his men."

"But how do we make this happen?" Jaleh ruminated. "It will not be in our hands, but in the hands of the agent."

"Put the idea in his head, Madame Jaleh," Nasim suggested. "You are never afraid to speak up. He will want the matter settled quickly so he can be done with it and get his commission."

"Nasim is right, *Ema*," Parvaneh said excitedly. "The agent will be happy to try to arrange something for all of us together. It will make his job easier."

Jaleh sat back, a faraway look on her face. "Imagine me cooking in the palace," she said dreamily.

"A very interesting picture," Behrooz said from the courtyard doorway. "I like that idea…."

They all jumped and turned to look at him. "Away!" Jaleh ordered, flapping her hand at him. "We have enough problems without you bothering us. I have no job here anymore. I have nothing to give you."

Behrooz sauntered into the kitchen, ignoring her words. "So the rumors I heard are true: that your great captain's life was snuffed out in Greece and that his privileged little daughter was carted off by her relatives." He surveyed the room and commented with satisfaction, "You are left here alone now putting things in order."

"We are not alone," Jaleh said quickly, rising from the table and confronting him. "An agent is on his way to go through the house."

"Then I came just in time, did I not?" he taunted. "Come, dear Jaleh, take me on a private tour before the agent arrives."

"No!" she cried. "The *daeva* take you! Everything here belongs to the captain and Monir."

Behrooz laughed. "The captain no longer needs anything where he is, and his daughter is far away with her relatives. Come, Jaleh," he said more insistently.

"I will not permit you to do this!" Jaleh cried, trying to push him from the room.

Nasim struggled to his feet to help her, grabbing Behrooz's arm, but suddenly the old man yelped and slumped back onto his stool, blood spurting from his forearm. Jaleh jumped back, giving Darya and Parvaneh a clear view of the knife in Behrooz's hand. The girls gasped and leaped up from their seats, not knowing what to do.

"Enough of this, Jaleh!" Behrooz warned in his gravelly voice, with no trace of the usual sinister smile on his face.

"Either you take me through the house, or I have my little talk with those two girls over there."

Jaleh shot him a look of pure hatred, but said, "Come quickly. You must be gone before the agent arrives."

"*Ema*, do not go with him!" Parvaneh cried out, as her mother began leaving the room with Behrooz.

"It will be all right," Jaleh assured her. "This dog will not bite me." She fixed her eyes on Behrooz until the force of her glare made him slowly sheathe his knife. Then she told the girls, "Both of you stay here and help Nasim."

Parvaneh and Darya watched fearfully as Jaleh and Behrooz left the kitchen, then they brought a bowl of water and some rags to the table to clean and bind the gash on Nasim's arm.

The three of them were not sure what to do next. Should they follow Jaleh to make sure she was all right, even though she had ordered them not to? They debated the idea for a few minutes until they were halted by the sound of someone ringing the bell that hung at the front gate.

"The agent!" Parvaneh exclaimed in panic. "He will see Master Behrooz going through the house. He will ask questions. He will think *Ema* cannot be trusted."

"The end of our dreams of working in the palace," Nasim muttered darkly, nursing his arm at the table.

Darya's heart pounded, but she said as calmly as she could, "Parvaneh, run to tell your mother that the agent is here. I will walk to the gate as slowly as I can. She must get Master Behrooz out the kitchen door before he is seen."

It seemed like a good plan, and it would have worked had Behrooz not been slowed by the bulging sack of booty that he insisted on hauling through the house with him as he made his exit. Although Darya dragged her feet as she led the agent into the central courtyard to wait for the housekeeper, he caught a glimpse of Behrooz and his sack struggling into the kitchen with Jaleh hurrying him along.

"What goes on here?" the agent demanded, brushing past Darya and confronting Jaleh and Behrooz.

The housekeeper's face went deathly pale while Behrooz laid down the sack. As he turned around slowly to face the agent, Darya could see his hand reaching stealthily for the knife in his belt. She was about to scream to warn the agent when, strangely, Behrooz's hand dropped to his side and his sinister smile spread across his face.

"So it is you, Kansbar," Behrooz said. "Hiring out as an agent."

The other man crossed his arms in front of his chest. "Behrooz, eh? I do not need to ask what *you* are doing these days."

∞

Darya could not believe it when, two weeks later, she, Jaleh, Parvaneh, and even Nasim, climbed into an open cart with Kansbar for the ride to the palace. After the captain's death, Monir's departure, and the near disaster with Behrooz, it had begun to seem to Darya that nothing good would ever come her way again; but here she was, saved from the slave market, surrounded by her friends, and riding toward King Xerxes' provincial home in Susa.

It had all come about so strangely that Jaleh had no doubt the *ahura* were looking out for them. How else could it be that the agent hired by Monir's uncle would once have been business partners with Behrooz, but certainly not involved in honest business, Jaleh insisted. When the two men had recognized each other, they had gone off together to the kitchen courtyard, where they talked privately for some time.

"They are up to no good," Jaleh had whispered to Nasim and the girls as the four of them sat once more around the kitchen table.

"What do we do?" Nasim asked, but no one had any suggestions. They sat glumly waiting, not knowing what was in store for them.

It came as a surprise, therefore, when the two men entered the room and Behrooz announced that Kansbar would attempt to have the four worried people placed at the palace.

"My friend Kansbar has connections," Behrooz told them gleefully. "His cousin is the King's chamberlain in charge of hiring servants and buying slaves—and his cousin owes him a favor."

The information was greeted with silence as the four people around the table tried to figure out what trap Behrooz might by laying for them. It simply could not be possible that one such as he could be trying to arrange the very thing they had all been praying for.

"Why are you doing this?" Jaleh demanded bluntly, speaking for all of them.

"Oh, Jaleh, Jaleh." Behrooz laughed, coming to the table and placing a hand on her shoulder that she roughly slapped away. "You must learn to be more trusting. I heard you talking before, when I first arrived. I know you are in need of work, these slaves must be sold, and all of you want to stay together. As I said before, I like the idea of you in the palace. I am only trying to help."

"Like a leopard helps his prey!" Jaleh muttered.

"Madame Jaleh," Kansbar said. There was a note of authority in his voice, and they all turned toward him. He was leaning against the doorway leading into the rest of the house. He was even taller and broader than Behrooz, and he commanded attention. "Whether or not you trust my friend Behrooz is no concern of mine. I was hired to do a job here, and this is the best way I see fit to do it. Your approval is not needed."

"Of course, sir," Jaleh replied stiffly. "I meant no disrespect, sir."

"Now, come show me around the house. Then I expect you and the slaves to start putting everything in top order for the sale while I visit my cousin at the palace."

Nine

Kansbar informed them three days later that Jaleh had indeed been hired as a cook, Parvaneh had been hired as a handmaiden for the women, and Nasim and Darya had been bought as slaves.

"We must thank the *ahura* for our good fortune," Jaleh told the girls that night as they prepared for sleep. "We must also be on our guard, because I have no doubt that Behrooz has something in mind—something evil—but no matter. We must be thankful that we have been granted our wish."

And now here they all were, in the wagon on the way to the palace. Jaleh and Parvaneh wore their best dresses, with Parvaneh's butterfly shawl wrapped proudly around her shoulders. Even Darya and Nasim felt well dressed, or at least better dressed than they had ever been in the captain's house.

Jaleh had ordered them to haul bucket after bucket of water from the neighborhood cistern to fill the large iron tub that stood behind a screen in the kitchen courtyard. Only the captain and Monir had ever used it, but now each of them bathed in turn. The cold water was dark and soupy by the time Darya sank into it after everyone else was through, but she was delighted by how cool and refreshed it made her feel.

When Parvaneh suggested they both untangle and smooth their hair with one of the brushes Monir had left behind, Darya felt positively royal. And the feeling escalated heavenward when Jaleh told her to wear Parvaneh's work tunic instead of her own coarse clothing. She could see that Nasim felt the same way when Jaleh gave him trousers and an old tunic of the captain's that had not been worth selling.

"We are moving to the palace," Jaleh had said proudly, "where even servants and slaves must look their best."

The four of them sat on the floor of the wagon behind Kansbar, gazing about them at the sights of the city as though they were people of means on an outing, rather than servants and slaves on their way to a new master.

The autumn day was fine, with a pleasant breeze from the west carrying the scents and sounds of the busy River Shaur. The captain's villa was situated near the southern wall of the city, so to reach the palace in the north, the wagon had to maneuver through the crowded food market stalls where Jaleh had always shopped, and the neighboring slave market that made Darya's chafed neck burn beneath the iron collar.

She peeked over the side of the wagon at the slave dealers hawking the merchandise displayed under their awnings and glimpsed a small group of children tied together, their eyes wide and fearful as hers must have been six years ago. Instinctively, Darya's fingers searched the folds of

Parvaneh's dress that she wore, looking for the precious *daric* she had tucked into it—the seed that might eventually sprout into a dream of freedom. *You are not being sold away to strangers*, she reminded herself, taking a calming breath. *You have Jaleh and Parvaneh and Nasim.*

But Darya did not feel safe until the slave market was behind them and a steep hill came into view topped by the fire-altar of *Ahura Mazda*. She could see Jaleh moving her lips in a silent prayer of thanks, and she too looked toward the top of the hill, where *magi* were tending the Sacred Fire. "Dear *ahura*," Darya whispered in her usual confused manner. "If I have the right to pray to you—if I am one of those that you look after—I thank you."

They entered a finer part of the city, and, not long afterward, the fortified wall that surrounded the palace loomed before them, tall, massive, and magnificent. Kansbar drove the wagon along the street beside the wall, passing guard stations at intervals, and Darya craned her neck to see how far it extended.

"It goes on forever," Parvaneh murmured. "Where is the entrance gate?"

"Not on this side," Jaleh told her. "We will be there soon."

And they were, after they rounded the corner to the eastern wall. The great square before the palace bustled with grand carriages, rough wagons, draped sedan chairs carried by slaves, and people on foot moving in all directions—entering the palace, leaving the palace, visiting fine residences and shops. Kansbar carefully guided his donkey toward the line of vehicles and sedan chairs waiting to enter the palace gate.

"This will take some time," he said over his shoulder. "The soldiers guarding the gate are never in any rush. The scribes on duty check people's documents, and the soldiers ask questions and search vehicles. And a wagon such as ours gets pushed to the side if a fine carriage drives up demanding entrance."

The four in the wagon had plenty of time to absorb the sights of the square before they moved to the head of the line. What fascinated Darya most was the variety of people. As expected, there were bearded Persian men wearing tall felt *kulahs* on their heads, and even some with fancier ribbed hats called *kidaris*. They draped fine coats over their shoulders, partially covering their tunics and trousers. And there were Persian women, demurely veiled for the outdoors, wearing long, colorful capes over tunics and skirts. They were attended by female servants and slaves, who were banned from veiling their faces, as Darya and her female companions were banned, to ensure that no one mistook them for women of a higher class. But besides all the Persians, it seemed as though every land in the world was represented by visitors to the royal square.

"I wish I knew more about the world," Darya said to Parvaneh, "so I would know where all these people are from. Like that group over there," she said, pointing to three men in long, brightly colored coats over trousers that reached to their ankles. They wore round caps instead of *kulahs*, and their dark eyes were shaped like almonds.

"*Ema*, do you know where they are from?" Parvaneh asked her mother.

Jaleh shook her head. "I can tell they are foreign, but I do not know their country."

"It is a place called Cin," Nasim said, to everyone's amazement. "Their country is far to the east of the Empire, but they come here to trade. They bring spices and so much silk that their trade route is called the Silk Road."

"Like the dress worn by Monir's aunt," Parvaneh remembered, making Darya shudder at the thought of her.

"How would you know all that, Nasim?" Jaleh demanded. It obviously annoyed her that the old slave possessed a greater font of knowledge than she. "Just using your eyes and ears again?"

"I told you I was once a merchant," Nasim explained proudly. "Long ago, in Persepolis. I dealt with foreigners all the time. I had to know who they were and where they were from. I even had to know what kinds of food they ate so I would know what to serve them."

Further conversation was cut short by their arrival at the palace gate. After a scribe checked Kansbar's documents—the purchase order from his cousin, the King's chamberlain, written on a papyrus scroll—the soldiers ordered everyone out of the wagon and examined it carefully. They asked for names and ages and had the scribe check them against the document.

"I do not remember going through all this checking last time I had dealings with the palace," Kansbar remarked to one of the soldiers.

"Orders, sir," the soldier responded curtly. "The King is in residence. Plots have been uncovered."

"I see," Kansbar said, helping Jaleh back into the wagon. "A result of the war, I suppose," he murmured to himself. "People who are not happy with the outcome."

"Did I not tell you?" Nasim whispered to Jaleh. "The war was not a success."

"Hush," Jaleh warned. "We are entering the palace."

The wagon passed before a giant, brightly painted statue of a proud man wearing a crown and regal robes that made them all feel small and insignificant. "That is great King Darius," Kansbar said softly, over his shoulder. "That statue used to stand in Egypt to show that we Persians conquered it, and the writing on the platform below his feet lists all the lands of the Empire."

Darya craned her neck, attempting to read the chiseled writing, but it was neither Aramaic nor Persian. "The writing is done in their strange picture alphabet," Kansbar continued. "If I remember correctly, it is called hieroglyphs."

Darya would have loved to hear more about it—and she felt a sudden sharp longing to be sitting next to Saeed and Monir again, learning how to decipher written words—but the view of the statue was cut off as they entered the palace gates. The entrance passageway twisted and turned, forcing Kansbar to guide the donkey slowly and carefully.

"Why would they build an entrance this way?" Parvaneh asked. "So difficult to get through."

"Just so," Kansbar told her, concentrating on driving the donkey. "If an enemy wanted to attack the palace, he could not burst in quickly, could he?"

"Do people live in these walls, Master Kansbar?" Darya asked, noticing doors embedded in the walls of the passageway. She spoke hesitantly, not sure how Kansbar would react to a slave girl's question.

But Kansbar replied easily, as he had to the others. "No," he said. "But special people—advisors to the King, people of high rank, representatives of different groups—have offices here. This is the King's Gate."

As they watched, two men emerged from one of the doors. They walked through the passageway, deep in conversation. Both wore tunics and trousers like other Persian men, but instead of tall Persian hats, they wore close-fitting skullcaps. And something else about them was different. It set them apart. At last Darya realized what it was.

"Their hair and beards," Darya said. "They do not look Persian. They are not trimmed and curled in the Persian style."

"Those men are Hebrews—Judeans, from the western edge of the Empire, along the coast of the Great Sea," Nasim said. "There are many in Susa. They dress like Persians, but they have their own ways that set them apart. Instead of praying to *Ahura Mazda* and all the other *ahura*, they worship only one God."

"And you know that from your days as a merchant, I'm sure," Jaleh said caustically.

"Yes, Madame Jaleh," Nasim replied evenly. "I had to be very careful what food I served the Judeans. Their religion has many rules laid out in a scroll they call a *Torah*. It makes them very particular about what they eat."

At last the wagon was inside the walls. It was like entering another world. The four passengers were bombarded by the hues and the perfumes of a huge, carefully laid out garden, the likes of which none of them had ever imagined existed. It overwhelmed them, but then they looked up to see the palace rising and extending spectacularly behind it.

It sat regally upon a terraced hill that accentuated the building's height and breadth, as one magnificent level rose behind another like mountain peaks reaching for the heavens. No one spoke. They did not exclaim or point. They simply stared, trying to comprehend the immensity and the glory of what lay before them, attempting to absorb it with their senses and grasp it with their minds.

Kansbar stopped the wagon and glanced back at his passengers. "I can see none of you has ever been here before," he said with a smile, noting their wide eyes and open mouths, "or seen a garden like this—a *paradaisia*." It occurred to Darya that this man might be a friend of Behrooz, but his personality was very different. He never spoke harshly to any of them, and he obviously took pleasure in telling them about their surroundings.

"I can only imagine your faces if I were taking you to the palace in Persepolis instead of this one," Kansbar remarked.

"It cannot possibly be more magnificent than this," Jaleh breathed.

"Oh, but it is, Madame Jaleh," Kansbar replied. "Or at least it will be, when it is fully completed. Remember, Persepolis is the chief capital city of Persia, and the palace there lives up to that, especially because it is where the King celebrates *Novruz*, the coming of spring, and because it is the home of Queen Amestris. Susa is only a business capital, the place where the King runs the Empire."

"There is a queen in Persepolis, Master Kansbar?" Darya asked in confusion. "Then who was Queen Vashti?"

Kansbar laughed. "Do you think kings are like other men, with only one wife, or maybe two?"

"But all the women," Parvaneh said, as mystified as Darya. "The women gathered in the palace. Do they know of Queen Amestris?"

"Of course, child," Jaleh told her. "She is powerful, and known throughout the Empire."

Darya and Parvaneh exchanged amazed glances as Kansbar flicked the donkey's reins to start the wagon moving again. They followed a road through the *paradaisia* that eventually led them behind the palace to the kitchens and storerooms and laundry rooms and stables. It was a small city populated by workers like themselves, serving the larger city that was the palace, which sat ensconced within the great city of Susa, administrative capital of the grand Empire of Persia.

"Wait here," Kansbar ordered, jumping down from the wagon and striding toward a large storeroom. It was not long before he emerged with a man much older than he, but one who bore a strong family resemblance.

"Kansbar's cousin," Jaleh said softly. "Our new master."

Ten

"Can you see me?" Darya asked Parvaneh softly, late in the evening, two weeks after their arrival at the palace.

"Of course I can," Parvaneh responded just as quietly. "It is not yet fully dark."

"But do you see a person?" Darya insisted.

"What do you mean?" Parvaneh asked in confusion. "Of course you are a person."

"Good." Darya laughed half-heartedly. "Then I am not truly invisible. I only feel that way working here day after day."

The two girls had hardly seen each other since they had come to the palace. They did not work together or sleep together, and since the compound was so large, they rarely crossed paths. They were only together now because Parvaneh had been able to get away from her duties for an hour. She had sought out Darya in the female slave barracks, and the two girls had made their way outside to sit on discarded wooden barrels placed near the wall of the slave quarters. They kept their voices low so as not to attract attention, which would likely lead to one or both of them being ordered to do some task.

"Why do you feel invisible?" Parvaneh asked.

"No one ever looks at me or talks to me," Darya sighed, "except in the morning, when Golnar, the head slave, assigns the jobs, and at night when she makes sure I get the last food stuck to the bottom of the pots, and that I sleep in a corner where no one else wants to be."

"What set her against you?" Parvaneh asked.

Darya shrugged. "I did nothing but step into the slave barracks when we first came here, and she was upon me. Everyone fears her, except her favorites, who get the easiest jobs and the pick of the food. I have heard whispers that no one knows her real name or what country she came from. Her first Persian master called her Golnar—they say it means 'fire'—because of the color of her hair, and that is the name she uses." Darya shook her head sadly. "Except for her, I go about my work like a shadow. No one bothers to look at me when I move about. It is as if I am not there, as if some invisible spirit was doing the work."

"What do you do?" Parvaneh asked.

"Can you not smell it on my clothes?" Darya asked.

Parvaneh leaned toward her friend and sniffed, then wrinkled her nose. "What is it?"

"Chamber pots," Darya replied in disgust. "All day, every day. On my first morning, Golnar sent me to that giant shed over there at the back gate." Darya nodded toward a building not far away. "Sometimes she sends two of us, but often it is just me. It is where the chamber pots are brought from all over the palace. I empty the night soil into a water trough that runs through the building. Then I wash the pots with boiling water so they will be ready to go back to everyone's rooms late in the afternoon." She rubbed her forehead as though it pained her. "Hundreds every day," she murmured. "The only good thing is that the shed is near the stables, and once in a while I see Nasim."

Parvaneh was silent. Finally, she said softly, "But you used to do almost the same thing for everyone at the captain's house."

"There were only a few pots," Darya replied. "And all of you looked at me. You talked to me. Monir and I—we played together and learned together and—" Her voice caught and she stopped, then looked sadly at Parvaneh. "I miss them," she whispered. "The captain, Monir, our life there...."

"I know," Parvaneh sympathized. "I do too."

Darya took a deep breath and gazed up at the first stars glittering in the darkening sky. "What do *you* do all day?" she asked Parvaneh. "You told me you help your mother in the kitchens and that you were also assigned to one of the women waiting to meet the King. How do you do both?"

Parvaneh hesitated. "My lady is named Esther," she mumbled, weaving her fingers together nervously. "She is lovely and kind and soft-spoken."

She broke off and Darya repeated, "How do you have time to also work in the kitchens?"

"I am not supposed to say," Parvaneh murmured guiltily, not meeting Darya's eyes. "My lady made me promise."

"I do not understand," Darya said. "You may not speak about your work for your lady?"

Parvaneh nodded.

"But it seems you do not work for your Lady Esther all the time or you would not be able to also work for Madame Jaleh. Is that not so?"

After a moment, Parvaneh nodded quickly. "Remember, I did not tell you that," she said nervously. "You figured it out for yourself."

Darya stared at her friend. "If your lady is so lovely and kind, why do you look so frightened?"

Parvaneh bit her lip. "This is the palace," she said in a hushed voice. "Things go on here. People whisper in corners. If my lady made me promise to be silent, I must be silent."

"Yes, you must be silent!" came a harsh voice from the doorway of the slave barracks. Both girls jumped up guiltily from the barrels and faced a huge woman with flaming red hair who was carrying a stout wooden rod.

"Golnar," Darya hissed to Parvaneh.

"Two ladies of leisure," the woman taunted, "relaxing in the evening air. You!" she said sharply, poking Parvaneh with the rod. "Back to your duties. And you!" she barked at Darya, swinging the rod so that it would have hit Darya's shoulder had she not jumped out of reach. "Someone just vomited in here. Get a bucket of water and some rags and clean it up so we will not be smelling it all night!"

With one last pitying look over her shoulder, Parvaneh hurried off in the direction of the women's quarters, while Darya rushed in the opposite direction—away from the rod—toward a water cistern and buckets.

Eleven

The girls did not see each other again for two more weeks, by which time Darya's face, arms and legs were discolored with large purple bruises from encounters with Golnar's rod.

"Are you all right?" Parvaneh asked her friend with concern. This time the two girls were crouching on the ground behind the slave barracks, hoping to avoid detection. But even in the fading light, Parvaneh could see the fear in Darya's eyes.

"She will kill me before she is through," Darya whispered, shivering in the chill evening air. "It does not matter what I do or say—she takes pleasure in beating me. She uses me to keep the other slaves afraid of her."

"I will talk to my mother," Parvaneh said softly. "She will know what to do. Sometimes Kansbar's cousin, Master Arman, comes into the kitchens. She will talk to him."

Darya shook her head. "Why would he care about a slave? He put Golnar in charge here so he would not need to be bothered with us. If this is the way she does her job, he would not want your mother to trouble him about it."

"But he paid golden *darics* for you. He would not want you hurt this way for no reason," Parvaneh argued.

Darya's shoulders slumped. "They were not his own *darics* that he paid. And there are so many slaves and servants here. One more or less will not matter to him."

The girls sat silently on the ground side by side until Parvaneh exclaimed softly, "Oh! I almost forgot why I came here this evening. I was so upset to see your bruises that I forgot to give you this." Rummaging in the folds of her tunic, she pulled out a small papyrus scroll and held it out to Darya.

"What is it?" Darya asked in surprise, staring at the scroll.

"One of the guards brought the post to the women's quarters today. He brings it there twice every week. Many of the women are far from home, and their families write to them. He calls out their names, and the handmaidens fetch the scrolls for them, although my Lady Esther has never received one."

"Why did you bring this scroll here?" Darya asked in confusion.

"Because it is not for one of the women—it is for you. From Mistress Monir!"

Darya's expression registered shock and then pure pleasure, which was mirrored on Parvaneh's face as she handed the scroll to her friend.

"The guard kept calling out, 'Lady Darya,'" Parvaneh laughed, "but no one stepped forward for the scroll until, finally, it occurred to me that perhaps 'Lady Darya' was you!"

The girls giggled delightedly, then stood and looked around in search of a place that was light enough for reading.

"Over there," Parvaneh said softly, pointing to a lamp whose flame lit up the path that led to the stables.

"Golnar might see us there," Darya said fearfully. "We can see that torch from the entrance of the slave barracks."

"How about behind those?" Parvaneh suggested, indicating some empty wooden barrels that had been left lying near the path. "We can hide behind them and still get some light from the lamp."

Darya remained fearful, but the scroll was too tempting. She needed so much to read what Monir had written and to be reminded of the warmth of living with people who cared about her. Hesitantly, she crept with Parvaneh toward the barrels and crouched behind them. Then, with trembling fingers, she broke the seal on the scroll and unrolled the papyrus.

"What does it say?" Parvaneh hissed urgently, as Darya scanned the writing.

"It is hard to read in this light," Darya said. "And Mistress Monir's writing is not clear. I think she is beginning to forget what Master Saeed taught her." She peered at the scroll. "It says, *My Dear Darya,*" she began. "*I wanted to write to you for so long, but my*—I think this says *my aunt,*" Darya said, glancing at Parvaneh—"*but my aunt kept forgetting to ask the servants to buy ink and papyrus for me.*"

"Her aunt kept 'forgetting,'" Parvaneh repeated sarcastically, and Darya nodded knowingly.

"But now I am writing to you," Darya continued, *"only it is so*—I think she wrote *so hard. It is so hard because I have forgotten so many of Master Saeed's lessons.* Just like I told you," Darya said, glancing at Parvaneh again. *"Persepolis is a very busy city,"* Darya read, struggling with the strange name, *"and my uncle's house is busy too. He always has visitors because he is a merchant."*

"That is like what Nasim told us," Parvaneh put in. "Remember? When he told us about when he used to be a merchant?"

Darya nodded. *"I miss my home in Susa,"* she carried on, haltingly. *"Please tell Madame Jaleh, Parvaneh, and Nasim that I miss them terribly. But my cousin Mehrdad tries to make me feel better. He is the boy who is my age. My older cousins do not pay any attention to me."*

"At least she has Mehrdad," Parvaneh said, peering at the scroll. "But show me where Mistress Monir wrote my name. I want to see how it looks."

Both girls were leaning over the scroll as Darya pointed to Parvaneh's name, when suddenly Golnar's rod smashed between them, bruising their arms and tearing the letter from Darya's hand.

"Always sneaking off!" Golnar shouted, swinging the rod wildly as Darya and Parvaneh cried out and tried to scramble out of reach. "What are you doing out here? What are you two plotting?"

"Nothing," Darya protested, desperately trying to retrieve the precious scroll before Golnar trampled it beneath her feet. "It is only a letter from my young mistress. She wrote to me from Persepolis."

"You lie!" Golnar bellowed, thumping the rod down on Darya's shoulder and grabbing the scroll out of her hands. "No mistress writes to a slave. You are up to no good. Whose scroll do you have?"

"It is mine," Darya insisted, reaching for the papyrus, only to have her hand whacked away by the rod. "Please, Miss Golnar," she begged, nursing her bruised hand with the other one. "Let me show you my name. I will read to you where my mistress wrote my name on the letter."

Golnar stood suddenly still, one hand raised with the rod poised to swing down, the other clutching the scroll. "You will read it to me?" she echoed incredulously. "Do you take me for a fool? You will point at the scroll, and say some words, and expect me to believe that you are reading?"

The rod smashed into Darya's shoulder and neck, clanging against her slave collar and knocking her to the ground, while blow followed blow.

"Stop! You will kill her!" Parvaneh screamed in horror. She saw slaves cramming the doorway of their barracks, staring at the awful scene, and some stablemen hurrying out to see what was causing the commotion.

"Please! Someone stop her!" Parvaneh begged. But no one moved except for one stableman, who hurried off toward the storehouses. Desperately, Parvaneh flung herself at Golnar, trying to grab the lethal rod, but the giant woman tossed her away like a dung cake and Parvaneh landed hard among the barrels. Scrambling up, she saw the beating continue, and not knowing what else to do, she simply screamed—over and over, as long and as loud as she could.

Twelve

"What goes on here?!" came an authoritative male voice. "Golnar! What is this all about?"

Swinging the rod down one last time across Darya's form, now unmoving on the ground, Golnar turned toward the path where Master Arman, Kansbar's gray-bearded cousin, stood near the lamp post, with Nasim right behind him. Only then did Parvaneh realize that Nasim was the stablehand who had run off and that he had fetched the King's chamberlain. Golnar's eyes seemed glazed over, and spittle dripped from her open mouth. She breathed heavily until her mind finally seemed to clear and she panted, "Forgive me, Master Arman … for all the noise…. These girls were plotting…. They stole a scroll…. They were hiding behind those barrels over there … I was trying to find out what they were planning."

"Over here, girl," Arman ordered Parvaneh. Trembling, she stepped away from the barrels and stood before him. "Where did you get that scroll?"

"From one of the guards, Master," she replied in a quavering voice, her heart pounding. "In the women's quarters."

"Why did he give it to you?" he demanded.

"He thought it was for a lady named Darya, Master," Parvaneh tried to explain, her voice still shaking. "But there is no Lady Darya in the women's quarters. He kept calling out her name, until I thought of my friend—" Parvaneh glanced worriedly at Darya, lying motionless on the ground.

"She is called Darya?" Arman inquired of Golnar, who nodded her head, and from behind him, Nasim said, "That is her name, Master."

"So you brought her the scroll," Arman said, turning back to Parvaneh.

"Yes, Master," she replied. "We were only reading it— *Darya* was reading it—that is all we were doing. We were not plotting. We—"

"She is lying!" Golnar broke in. "No slave girls can read. And no mistress would write to a slave. That is why I was beating her—for lying. I wanted the truth!"

"You say your friend Darya over there was reading the letter." Arman was addressing Parvaneh and pointing to the figure on the ground. Parvaneh nodded. "All right, then, girl, tell me what it says."

Parvaneh took a shaky breath and Golnar smirked. "Yes, girl, tell the master what it says."

Parvaneh glanced at Nasim for courage, then said, "It is from our young mistress, Monir." She stopped to try to organize her thoughts. "Oh yes—she said that her aunt kept forgetting to buy her papyrus and ink, but Darya and I do not think her aunt forgot, Master, we think—"

"Just tell me what the scroll says, girl," Arman barked impatiently. "I do not have all night to waste here!"

"Yes, Master," Parvaneh said quickly. "Mistress Monir wrote that Persepolis is busy, and her uncle's house is busy—and her younger cousin is nice to her, but her older cousins do not pay attention to her, and she misses all of us, even me and Nasim over there, she wrote our names on the scroll, and—"

"Enough, girl!" Arman commanded. "Golnar, hand me the letter."

The head slave held out the creased and torn papyrus scroll. After unrolling it, Arman scanned it quickly in the light from the lamp. "This is no plot, Golnar," he said, and Parvaneh let out her breath. "This is a child's letter."

"But, Master, how could I know that?" Golnar protested. "I had to be sure—to protect the palace."

"Just so," Arman agreed. "But next time, call for one of the scribes to read the letter, instead of beating one of the King's slaves to death."

"She is dead?" Parvaneh cried, dropping to her knees beside Darya. "She cannot be. No!" Gently, Parvaneh stroked Darya's hair, which was matted with blood, while Nasim came forward and crouched next to her.

"She is not dead, Master Arman," Golnar objected. "I know better than to destroy the King's property. The girl will be up and ready to work in the morning, I swear to you, even if I have to drag her—"

"No, Golnar," Arman cut in. "You will not touch her in

the morning. By the looks of it, she will need at least a day to recover. Send someone else to do her work."

"As you wish, Master," Golnar said reluctantly. "But if it was up to me, I would not coddle her."

"It is not up to you, Golnar," Arman replied firmly. "You over there," he said to Nasim. "Get the girl into the barracks and leave her be. And Golnar, get all these slaves back where they belong."

The head slave began to shoo everyone back to the barracks and the stables, while Parvaneh watched worriedly as Nasim struggled to lift Darya in his arms. But the old slave did not move toward the barracks when he was finally upright. Instead he turned toward Arman.

"Master," he said hesitantly, "the girl is badly hurt. She might need some care. Perhaps I should take her some-place else."

Arman looked from the unconscious Darya to Golnar, who was prodding slaves roughly with her rod. "You might be right, old man," he said. "But where can we put her?"

Nasim was at a loss, but Parvaneh said quickly, "Perhaps my mother's room—Madame Jaleh, in the kitchens. She knows Darya. She will know what is needed."

Arman nodded, obviously pleased that a solution had been found so quickly. "Take her to the kitchens and find Jaleh," he told Nasim, who hastily carried Darya away before Golnar might notice and try to change Arman's mind.

Parvaneh watched them go, then glanced toward Arman, not knowing if he was done with her and if she should return to the women's quarters.

"You, girl," he said. "Tell me, how is it that the slave girl could read that scroll?"

"She was taught, Master," Parvaneh replied. "Together with our Mistress Monir. So that she could help her with her studies."

"And why was your Mistress Monir learning to read?" Arman asked curiously.

"Our master—her father—he wanted it. He was an army captain who was killed in Greece. He wanted his daughter to know how to read. He thought it would help her to take care of herself, if she ever needed to."

"Ahh," Arman said. "Your master was the army captain who was killed. You came here with my cousin Kansbar— four of you."

"Yes, Master," Parvaneh replied. She added quickly, "We are all loyal. We are not plotters."

"Who is your lady in the women's quarters?" he asked.

"The Lady Esther, Master."

"Hmm," Arman mused. "The secretive Lady Esther. I have heard of her." He gazed at Parvaneh sharply, making her uncomfortable. "Is your Lady Esther a plotter, girl?"

"Certainly not, Master," Parvaneh replied hastily, taken aback. "She is wonderful."

But Arman continued to appraise her. "You have a good head on your shoulders, girl. I like the way you answer all my questions and the way you stand up for your friend and your lady." His voice dropped and he said almost to himself, "I can use someone like you—and someone like your friend, who can read."

His dark eyes bored into Parvaneh, who stood before him uneasily. "I want you to check on your friend tomorrow and for the next few days. Tell your mother that when Darya is ready, she should set her to work in the kitchens for the time being. I will send word to the Lady Esther that you are doing this for me, and I want you to report to me when Darya is well again. Here," he said, holding out the scroll, "give this back to your friend when you see her."

"Thank you, Master," Parvaneh replied gratefully, taking the scroll and thinking that Arman's authoritative yet fair attitude reminded her very strongly of his cousin Kansbar.

"And I want you to keep your eyes and ears open in the women's quarters," Arman continued. "Report to me if anything suspicious goes on there—with your Lady Esther, or anyone else."

"Certainly, Master," Parvaneh said, but she could no longer meet his eyes. When Arman finally allowed her to return to the women's quarters, Parvaneh kept wondering what he was looking for and what he wanted her to find out. It disturbed her that he had called the Lady Esther secretive. How much did she really know about her wonderful lady?

Thirteen

For Darya, waking up on the floor of Jaleh's room the next morning instead of in Golnar's slave barracks was like leaping out of the shadowy caverns of the *daeva* into the bright gardens of the *ahura*. Jaleh could not do enough for her, bringing Darya delectable foods lifted from trays on their way to the women's quarters, and chilled compresses for her bruises, made from rags soaked in the cold waters of the *kariz*, the trench that ran beneath the palace grounds and filled the *ab anbar*, the private reservoir that served the King. When Parvaneh told her mother that Arman wanted Darya to work in the kitchens temporarily, Jaleh beamed, then insisted that Darya could not possibly be well enough to work for at least three days.

"You are treating me like a noblewoman," Darya protested on the second morning, as Jaleh prepared to leave her room for the kitchens. "I should be going with you." But when Darya stood up, a wave of dizziness almost toppled her, and when she looked at Jaleh, the woman's face seemed hazy and blurred.

"You are not ready," Jaleh said with concern, grabbing Darya's arm and helping her sink to the floor again. "That witch should be flogged for what she did to you. It is a miracle that there are no broken bones."

"No one will punish Golnar," Darya murmured, gratefully lying down and massaging her forehead, which had begun throbbing painfully. "At least I am not in her barracks for the time being."

"I pray you will never go back there," Jaleh said, tucking a blanket around Darya before she left.

Jaleh's room was little more than a small closet off the kitchens, with a bit of light struggling through a high, tiny window, and just enough space for a pallet on the floor, but the quiet corner into which she had squeezed Darya was heavenly to the girl after the tumult and crowding of the slave barracks. Darya fell asleep again almost as soon as Jaleh left and did not wake until late afternoon, when Parvaneh came to check on her.

"My mother sent you food," Parvaneh said, placing a small tray on the floor. "It looks wonderful, and she made sure to send enough for both of us."

Darya lifted herself carefully to a sitting position, moving slowly to head off another wave of dizziness. She leaned her back against the wall and smiled at Parvaneh.

"It is like a picnic," Darya said. "Like when we used to have lunch in the courtyard together with Monir."

Parvaneh nodded and reached for a delicate pastry drizzled with honey. "Golnar must never know we are eating this way," she said, her mouth filled with splendid flavors and textures. "She would murder us."

Both girls giggled, but kept their voices low, still not quite certain that the giant slave would not barge into the room, her rod flailing.

"You know, you are famous now in the women's quarters," Parvaneh remarked, when they had eaten their fill.

"I am?" Darya said in surprise. "Why?"

"Because of Mistress Monir's scroll. You are the slave girl who can read! The women have all heard about you from the slaves and stablemen who saw the beating. And they are clamoring for you to come to the women's quarters."

"They are? For what reason?" Darya asked, mystified.

"To read them their letters," Parvaneh replied. "And to write their letters for them. I told you they receive scrolls from their families, but they need to wait for one of the palace scribes to have time to come to the women's quarters to read the letters to them. And when a scribe finally comes, they argue over whose letter will be read first or written first. Some of the women pay the scribes or give them gifts to get special treatment. The women have been complaining about it to Hegai, the head of the guards. They want him to bring you to the women's quarters to be a scribe just for them."

Darya stared at Parvaneh. "They truly want me in the women's quarters?" she asked in amazement. "Is it possible that might happen?"

Parvaneh nodded. "It just might. Hegai is powerful, and his job is to make all the women happy while they are waiting to meet the King. If this is what the women want, Hegai will try to get it for them."

Darya sat back against the wall, tears welling up in her eyes. She thought about not having to return to the slave barracks, or wash hundreds of soiled chamber pots, or be ruled by Golnar. It seemed too much to hope for. "Who is it that Hegai must convince to let me go there?" she asked in a small voice.

"I am not certain," Parvaneh replied. "But Kansbar's cousin, Master Arman, is the King's chamberlain in charge of the slaves." She smiled broadly and added excitedly, "Master Arman asked me to report to him when you were well enough to work again. And if I am not mistaken, I think he also wants you in the women's quarters!"

∞

Darya could not believe that any place on Earth could be more magnificent than the women's quarters. Parvaneh insisted that she had heard that the King's apartments were far more splendid, and that the *apadena*, his grand audience hall, was beyond imagining, with a carved cedar roof supported by thirty-six giant pillars topped by bulls' heads. But to Darya, the women's quarters were perfect, and how could anything surpass perfection?

After Darya had worked alongside Jaleh in the kitchens for a week, Master Arman summoned her to his office in one of the storehouses. He informed her that one of the Lady Esther's seven handmaidens had suddenly and mysteriously fallen ill and had immediately been removed from the palace to protect the health of the King and the women. Darya would take her place and, when she was not serving her lady, would be a scribe for all the women. She would also report to Master Arman on a regular basis, detailing the contents of the women's incoming and outgoing letters, and anything that seemed unusual or amiss in the women's quarters.

In a daze, Darya had followed Master Arman's orders to bathe in an iron tub in the kitchen courtyard—this time with water that was delightfully warm and fresh, having first been heated in a cauldron and having been prepared for Darya alone. Then she dressed in a neat and clean tunic that Master Arman gave her from one of the storerooms, and even untangled and smoothed her hair with a brush he issued to her.

Feeling like a newly crafted person, she reported to Hegai, the tall, shaven-headed chief of the guards, who led her into the dream world that was the women's quarters. Darya's bare feet were caressed by smooth marble floors that stretched below high, gilded ceilings that were inlaid with jewel-toned mosaics. The ceilings were supported by gleaming alabaster columns topped with carved swirls and rosettes. The air beneath was charmingly perfumed by flower-filled courtyard gardens, and cooled by breezes wafting in from the clever wind-catcher towers built into the roofs all over the palace. Exquisite fountains tinkled musically as water cascaded down artful arrangements of glistening stones. Rainbow-hued gossamer draperies rippled in the slightest puff of air, while graceful, gilded tables and chairs, and low, cushioned benches sparkled in the sunlight. And everywhere were the women, all of them young, each one lovelier than the one before.

They stood talking near the fountains, or sat at the tables or on overstuffed cushions, sipping chilled drinks. They worked on delicate embroidery, or played enchanting music upon lyres, or laughed at the antics of a monkey that one of the guards held on a leash, or applauded a juggler as he moved among the tables, tossing silver and golden balls into the air. Each woman was attended by handmaidens, bringing her whatever she called for, or massaging her delicate feet, or buffing the nails on her fine fingers, or brushing her shimmering hair.

Darya did not know where to look first, and was hard-pressed to keep her eyes on Hegai and follow him as he strode toward one of the chambers around the perimeter of the quarters. He knocked on a closed door that was promptly opened by a handmaiden.

"Is the Lady Esther about?" he inquired.

"Yes, sir," the girl responded, standing aside and allowing him to enter.

Hegai motioned to Darya to follow him, and he entered Esther's room.

The first thing Darya noticed was that Lady Esther was sitting at a table studying a scroll lying before her. *She can read!* Darya thought with pleasure. Then, when the young woman turned and stood to greet Hegai, Darya became aware of her loveliness—not so much classic beauty as an attractiveness that shone through her intelligent eyes, smiling lips, and welcoming stance.

"Master Hegai," she said in a musical voice. "How nice of you to visit me."

"I have come on business, Lady Esther," the guard said. "I have brought you a replacement for your seventh handmaiden."

"Ahh," Esther said, turning toward Darya and appraising her. "What is your name, child?"

"I am called Darya, My Lady," Darya replied with a curtsy, keeping her head respectfully lowered. But she was savoring the word "child" that Esther had used. It made her feel warm and protected, unlike other words people used for her, like "slave girl" or "lazy dog."

"How old are you, Darya?" Esther asked.

"I think I am twelve, My Lady, but I cannot be sure," Darya replied.

"Why is that?" Esther inquired.

"She is a slave girl, Lady," Hegai put in. "Many slaves have no way of knowing when they were born. But she comes to you highly recommended," he added quickly. "She is willing and loyal. And if you ever have any complaints about her, we will replace her immediately."

"I am sure I will have no complaints," Esther said, still looking at Darya. "But I do have a question. Look at me, child." Slowly, Darya raised her head. "Why is there an iron collar around your neck?" Esther asked.

Darya's face reddened. She lowered her eyes again, while

her hand automatically jumped to the collar and tried to pull it away from the side of her neck that was always chafed and was now bruised from Golnar's beating. "It is a slave collar, My Lady," Darya murmured almost inaudibly, feeling that she was not worthy to be standing in the same room as this lovely young woman.

Esther was silent for a few moments, then asked quietly, "What is its purpose?"

Darya thought back to her earliest memories. She did not want her new mistress to picture her as she once was, but she had no choice. She said hesitantly, "My first master—the man I remember as my first master when I was five or six— he used it to chain me to a wall so I could not run away."

Esther's eyes burned with anger, and she said in a tight voice to Hegai, "That collar must be removed if this child is to serve me."

"Certainly, Lady," Hegai replied with alacrity. "I will take her to the blacksmith immediately and it shall be done."

Within the hour the collar was gone. After more than six years of encircling Darya's neck, reminding her every minute, every day, of who she was, now, suddenly, it was just a twisted piece of metal lying on the floor of the palace smithy. Around Darya's neck now, besides the chafing and bruising, there was only a memory, a phantom that made her neck tingle because of the collar's absence. But in her heart, a seed of loyalty was sown, and a love for her new mistress that Darya felt might grow stronger than any metal wrought by man.

Fourteen

"You are always smiling these days," Parvaneh said to Darya, early one afternoon almost a month later.

Darya looked up from the letter she was penning to Monir. She sat at one of the gilded tables in a far corner of the women's quarters, a small stack of papyrus neatly piled before her, a pot of ink and a handful of sharpened reeds at the ready. The women were finishing lunch and would descend upon her in a moment with their letter-writing requests. In the meantime, she was snatching a few moments to tell Monir how her life had changed.

"I have so much to smile about," Darya responded. She laid down her reed and ticked off points on her fingers. "I spend time with you almost every day. Besides that, I am no longer in Golnar's slave barracks. I work for Lady Esther, the best of the women. I have clean clothes and good food." She stopped and the smile remained on her lips, but her eyes grew serious. "And I feel like a person."

"A person?" Parvaneh questioned. "What does that mean?"

"A person," Darya whispered. "Not a slave." She looked intently at her friend. "Do you notice how the women treat me?"

"Of course," Parvaneh replied. "I am here helping you all the time. They bring you their letters. They ask you to write to their families. They try to have you do their letters before someone else's. They bring you gifts...."

"Just so," Darya said. "They *ask* me for things. They bring gifts. Do you not see? They do not *order* me to do anything. They speak to me as they speak to each other— as they speak to other people."

"With respect," Parvaneh murmured softly, "because of your skill—your writing."

Darya nodded and tears filled her eyes. "Never before ... It has never been this way before."

Parvaneh thought for a minute. "I think it is also because most of them are not proud noblewomen, like we used to imagine. They are daughters of merchants and tradesmen."

"Why do you think that is so?" Darya wondered. "Why might the King not want a noblewoman for his next queen?"

Parvaneh shrugged, then said slowly and in a whisper, "Perhaps because Queen Vashti was noble. Was she not a princess of Babylonia, granddaughter of their last king, who was conquered by King Cyrus? I have heard some of the women say that she refused to follow orders from King Xerxes. That is what enraged him and that is why he banished her. Perhaps the King does not want another such as she."

The girls considered this for a few moments, then Parvaneh asked, "Where do you put your things—the coins and trinkets? Your tunic must be growing very heavy."

Darya laughed. "I tried to sew enough folds in my tunic, but you are right—it was growing heavy. So I give everything to Lady Esther for safe-keeping. I trust her."

"As do I," Parvaneh agreed. She hesitated a moment. "But Master Arman does not. Have you noticed?"

Darya nodded. "He has made that very clear. When I reported to him last week, he kept asking about her, even when I said there was nothing to tell."

"It was the same for me," Parvaneh said.

Darya picked up the reed pen and fingered it nervously. "That is the one shadow in all this sunlight shining down on me: the reports to Master Arman. I feel like a cat scratching the hand that strokes it when I must tell him what I have read in the women's letters and what I have written to their families and what I have seen in Lady Esther's apartment. What is he looking for?"

"He must protect the King—especially now, when King Xerxes is spending time with each of the women. What if one of them is plotting against him?"

"I am certain Lady Esther is not plotting, and yet Master Arman suspects her more than anyone else."

Parvaneh nodded. "I know—because she is so secretive. She will not tell anyone about her family, or where she is from. No wonder he is suspicious."

"Well, then, why does he not send her away? There are so many women here. One less would not be missed, and Master Arman would be more at ease."

Parvaneh shook her head. "He cannot do that. The

command was for unmarried young women to be brought to the palace from all over the kingdom. They belong to the King now. One will be chosen to be the new queen, and the others ... the others...."

"The others will live in the women's quarters for the rest of their lives as part of the King's court." The two girls fell silent until Darya added softly, "Would you want that to be your fate? If you were one of these women, would you want to spend your life here?"

The girls gazed at the soft beauty surrounding them and Parvaneh smiled. "It is lovely. Why would I not want to live here or someplace like this? The women are given everything they want."

"Except freedom," Darya whispered. "They can never leave." She looked at Parvaneh and surprise crept into her voice. "In that way, they are just like me."

They turned toward the closed door of Esther's apartment and Parvaneh said, "I never thought of it that way. Do you think that is why she often looks sad? Do you think she would rather not be here?"

Darya shrugged. "She is different from the others. She rarely comes out of her room. She asks for nothing: no perfumes, no salves, no bath oils. She eats none of the fancy meats that are sent to her table. She gives no orders—"

"Except for two," Parvaneh interrupted. "That we go to the King's Gate to tell her Judean friend that she is well, and that we do not talk about the schedule she set up for her seven handmaidens."

Darya nodded. "It is strange that she wants only one of us to serve her each day, and we must never switch days with each other. She leaves us with so much free time."

"I, for one, will not complain about that," Parvaneh laughed.

"Did you mention it to Master Arman?" Darya asked. "And about her friend at the gate—Master Mordechai—did you mention him?"

Parvaneh shook her head. "Neither one seemed important—although I am sure Master Arman would find some way to use them against her. All we say to Master Mordechai time after time is that the Lady Esther is well. Nothing more. And as for the schedule of the handmaidens…" She giggled. "I did not want to risk having it change."

Darya nodded. "The same for me. But why do you think she does it? Why would it matter if I served her on the sixth day and you on the seventh? So it would be you lighting the oil lamps as the room darkened in the evening of the seventh day. It would not be me, but the lamps would still be lit."

Parvaneh looked confused. "You light the lamps in the evening when you serve her?" she asked.

"Of course," Darya replied. "A lady does not light her own lamps."

"But she does," Parvaneh replied. "She insists on it. When I serve her on the sixth day, I must be sure to leave the lighting of the lamps to her. I forgot once and began lighting them myself." She bit her lip. "It was the one time she ever became cross with me."

Darya's brow furrowed. It had never occurred to her that each handmaiden's day might be different. That might be why Esther did not want the girls sharing information with each other. But why? What was important about the differences? In her mind, she began examining everything Esther did from morning to night on the seventh day. "Does Lady Esther pray on the sixth day, when you serve her?" she asked Parvaneh.

Parvaneh nodded. "She prays like my mother does. She moves her lips and talks quietly to the *ahura*."

"How do you know she is praying to the *ahura*?" Darya asked.

"Who else would she pray to? They are the gods."

Darya shook her head. "They are the Persian gods, but is Lady Esther Persian? I asked her once if she was praying to the *ahura* and her answer was very strange. She said that she was praying to the creator of the world, and the name she used for the creator was not important."

"But that is *Ahura Mazda*," Parvaneh exclaimed, laughing a bit uncomfortably. "Why would she not use his name?"

Darya shrugged. "If she is not Persian…" She struggled to phrase her answer, but lunch was over and the first of the women approached the table, letter in hand.

"Good day, Darya," a dark-haired beauty with green eyes said pleasantly, holding out a papyrus scroll. "I hurried through lunch to get here first so I could listen to you read my letter in peace." As Parvaneh brought her a chair, the young woman handed Darya a glittering hairclip shaped like a rose. "This is for you," she said sweetly, "for all the time you will take, writing my return letter. I spent the entire morning thinking of all the things I want you to tell my family."

Fifteen

Dusk was falling when Darya completed the last of the scrolls. She handed it to a gentle young woman from Sardis, who had cried softly as she dictated her messages to her parents and younger sisters.

"I know I should not cry," the woman apologized. "My sisters are so jealous that I am here and they are at home. But I miss them so ... and I do not know when I will see them again."

"Perhaps they will visit, My Lady," Darya said softly.

"Yes, of course. They will visit," the woman reassured herself. She took a steadying breath and rummaged in her reticule for some coins that she pressed into Darya's hand. "Thank you for your work. You are a sweet girl, Darya."

When the woman had gone to the fountain in the center of the courtyard to sit with her friends, Darya and Parvaneh tidied the scrolls, ink, and reeds on the table.

"Quickly. We must hurry," Parvaneh admonished. "We must report to Master Arman before dark."

The girls grabbed their shawls and left the warmth and tranquility of the women's quarters to rush through the surrounding gardens and down the road to the kitchens and storehouses. Master Arman interviewed Parvaneh first, while Darya waited outside his office, shivering in the cold night air and feeling nervous and vulnerable. In the distance, the slave barracks were hulking like a stalking beast in the dusk. At any moment, Golnar might appear. Perhaps she also needed to report to Master Arman and would arrive before Darya could return to the sanctuary of the women's quarters. Golnar always struck first and asked questions later. Darya could still feel the crack of the head slave's rod across her neck and shoulders.

She longed for the safety of Master Arman's office, but at the same time she dreaded it. She would tell him of the Sardis girl's tears and unhappiness, feeling as though she were betraying her. She would tell him that Lady Esther continued to spend her time reading scrolls that she borrowed from the palace library, detailing the history of the Persian Empire. Would that endanger Lady Esther in any way? How would Master Arman interpret the information? Darya could not bear to think that she might be hurting her lady.

At last Darya and Parvaneh traded places and Darya suffered through Master Arman's interrogation, feeling as guilty and fearful as she had anticipated.

"Darya!" Master Arman said sharply, and Darya sucked in her breath.

"Yes, Master?"

"Are you holding back information? Do you think you can only be loyal to the women you serve if you hide things from me?"

Darya felt as though his eyes were piercing her as she stood before his desk. "No!" she cried. "I mean, yes!" Darya began to tremble. "Oh, please, Master. I am not holding back information, but I do feel that I am not loyal to the women. And they are so kind to me." She looked at him pleadingly.

"Sit down," Arman said more calmly. Hesitantly, she perched on the edge of a chair as he stroked his gray beard and contemplated her. "Darya, are you loyal to the King?"

"Certainly, Master," she said tensely.

"Do you think I am loyal to the King?"

"Of course, Master!"

"Darya, loyalty means protecting the King from danger," he continued sternly. "When I question you, it is to protect the King. And your answers must be complete so you can help me protect the King. Do you understand?"

"Yes, sir," Darya whispered.

Arman was silent a moment, then asked, "Do you enjoy being in the women's quarters?"

"Oh, yes, Master!" she said fervently. "Thank you so much for sending me there."

His sharp eyes pierced her again. "You will remain there only if you are helpful to me. Do you understand? Golnar has been asking when you will return to the barracks."

Darya's heart pounded. "I understand, Master," she whispered.

At last, he dismissed her, and she joined Parvaneh outside.

"You are shaking," Parvaneh said.

Darya nodded. "Please, let us return to the women." She glanced around fearfully. "We are too close to Golnar. I could not bear to see her tonight."

They hastened down the path in the gathering winter darkness, but as they reached the first lamp post, a tall figure brushed past them, heading toward Master Arman's office. The girls continued walking but became aware that the figure had stopped abruptly behind them. Slowly, the girls halted and glanced over their shoulders.

"I thought it was you two," came a gravelly voice.

The girls' eyes widened in surprise and dismay as they stared into a familiar, sinister face. "Master Behrooz," Parvaneh whispered.

"One and the same," he responded, stepping closer to them, a joyless smile upon his lips. "Out and about, are you? Enjoying the evening air?"

"We are on our way to the women's quarters, sir," Parvaneh said tensely. "We work there."

"Both of you?" Behrooz questioned. "Even the slave girl?" He turned to Darya and eyed her neat clothing as she cringed away from him. "Coming up in the world, I see. What do you do there?"

"I serve the Lady Esther, sir," Darya mumbled, longing to run down the path.

"The Lady Esther … hmm … I have heard of her," Behrooz responded. "The secretive one." He glanced behind him toward Master Arman's office, then back to the girls. "So, Arman has you spying for him." He chuckled. "Sly old fox. He has everyone spying for him."

The girls were silent; then Parvaneh said, "We must go, sir. The Lady Esther expects us." She grabbed Darya's arm and began pulling her down the path.

"Go to your lady," Behrooz called after them, "but keep your eyes open. Next time I see you I just might have you report to me!"

His mirthless laughter chased them as the girls ran for the women's quarters.

Sixteen

"Oh! Forgive me, My Lady!" Darya cried out late in the afternoon two days later. She watched in horror as oil from the unlit lamp she had just knocked over stained the papyrus scroll Esther had been reading and dripped onto her skirt. Darya grabbed a cloth to dab at the liquid and tried to right the lamp, but her shaking hands sent the glass globe tumbling over the edge of the table and crashing to the floor.

"Oh! Oh..." Darya stared horrified at the mess, not knowing what to clean first. She began trembling and tears filled her eyes. "I am so sorry," she whispered. "I was only trying to light the lamp."

Esther reached over and gently pried the cloth from Darya's hand. Ignoring her stained skirt, she lifted the papyrus away from the oil spreading on the table, and laid the cloth across the liquid. "Sit down, Darya," Esther said quietly.

"But the glass ... the oil..." Darya stuttered.

"Sit down," Esther repeated.

Slowly Darya sank onto a chair near the desk. Her shoulders sagged and she stared at her hands in her lap.

"What is it, child?" Esther asked softly. "Something has been wrong all day. You look nervous ... frightened."

"It is nothing, My Lady," Darya mumbled. "My head has been aching. Forgive me. It will not happen again. Let me clean everything up." She began to rise from the chair.

"Sit," Esther said again, a note of sharpness in her voice. "I am not concerned about the oil or the lamp. I want to know why a girl who has been happy and competent ever since she started serving me is suddenly frightened and clumsy. Why, Darya?"

Darya bit her lip and would not raise her eyes.

"Answer me, child," Esther ordered.

Darya looked at her miserably. "Please, My Lady. I cannot say."

Esther's fingers drummed the table. She contemplated Darya for a few moments and finally seemed to come to a decision. "Child," she said, "the palace can be a dangerous place, and I have been very careful. But I trust you, and so I am going to tell you some things about myself that—"

"No, My Lady!" Darya almost shouted, cutting her off. She jumped up and covered her ears. "Do not tell me! I do not want to know. If I do not know, I cannot tell—" She broke off, horrified, realizing she had said too much.

But Esther only smiled. "Sit down, child," she said once more. "It is as I thought." As Darya sank onto the chair again, Esther continued, "You are being ordered to spy on me. Is that not so?"

Darya only stared at her, wide-eyed, not knowing what to say.

"There is no need to answer," Esther went on. "I know it

is true. I suspected as much when my seventh handmaiden took sick. It was so strange, so sudden. And then Hegai brought you to me—a slave who could read and write, for the only woman here who knows how to read and write— someone who was able to report on the reading and writing I was doing in my room all day."

"Forgive me," Darya whispered.

"Forgive you?" Esther asked kindly. "You are a slave. You are being threatened, are you not?"

Darya nodded almost imperceptibly.

"Of course you are," Esther continued. "You have no protection. If you do not do as you are told, you will be punished. What will they do to you? Beat you?"

Darya was silent but finally murmured, "I will be sent away from here—away from you and the other women." She clasped her hands tightly. "I will be sent back to the slave barracks, where the head slave almost killed me. And there is a man—another man who wants information." Darya shook her head and cried out, "Oh, My Lady, I am so afraid I will say something that will hurt you!"

"What you say cannot hurt me," Esther said soothingly, "because I am not doing or saying anything that can hurt the King."

"But you are secretive, My Lady," Darya said. "They do not trust you because you keep to yourself and no one knows who you are."

"Being secretive is not a crime," Esther replied. "If they are not comfortable with my silence, they can order me to leave. My silence is not something for you to concern yourself about, Darya. Is that clear?"

Slowly, Darya nodded.

"Do not fear for me, child," Esther continued. "Answer their questions truthfully. I want you to protect yourself. And if you are threatened with returning to the slave barracks, be sure to tell me. If it is in my power to help you, I will." She paused, then asked, "Is there anything else?"

Darya began to shake her head. She so much wanted to ask about the messages to the Judean, and why Parvaneh's tasks were so different from her own. And she wanted to know about Esther's prayers, whether she prayed to the Persian gods. But she was afraid. What if Esther gave her information that could hurt her with Master Arman? What if Esther grew angry that the girls had spoken about her? What if—

A knock on the door startled them both. The room had darkened around them as they spoke, the shattered lamp on the floor at their feet. Darya rose and opened the door to find Hegai on the threshold. He peered into the dim room, noticing the broken glass.

"Is everything all right, My Lady?" he asked Esther.

"Yes, of course," Esther responded with a smile, rising to greet him. "But I will need a new desk lamp."

"Certainly," Hegai responded. "And you will need much more than that. I am here to inform you that your time with the King begins in three days."

∞

Suddenly, everything began to move very quickly around Esther. For the first time, all seven of her handmaidens worked together, preparing Esther's baths, buffing her nails, brushing her hair, laying out her clothing. They had all seen this scenario take place multiple times in other rooms around the perimeter of the women's quarters, and they were prepared for endless demands from their mistress, but very few came. In fact, it was only at Hegai's prodding that Esther allowed oil of myrrh and perfumes to be poured into her bath water, and agreed to visit the storehouses and treasury with him to choose the gown and jewels she would wear.

"My Lady, it would not be respectful for you to appear before the King without proper clothing and jewels," he admonished her.

The handmaidens expected Hegai to leave them to their chores after that, and to reappear only when it was time for him to escort their lady to the King. But he hovered about, overseeing all of Esther's preparations, even coaching the girls in how to style her hair in a way that the King particularly liked.

"Hegai wants her to be the next queen," one of the girls whispered, and they all suddenly realized that she was right.

"We might all become the *Queen's* handmaidens!" a second girl almost squealed.

Darya only smiled. Her very special mistress might have much more in store for her than endless days in the women's quarters. And if she were queen, how much power and protection might she possess? It was almost too much to hope for.

Seventeen

"She walks like a queen," Parvaneh whispered, as the seven handmaidens watched Hegai escort Esther from the women's quarters on the evening of the third day. She seemed to glide across the marble floors, her jeweled dress and shawl draped elegantly and sparkling in the lamplight, her dark hair gleaming like a river in the night.

The bustle of the past three days abruptly ceased for the seven girls. They had bonded in their endeavor to make their lady the most beautiful of all who came before the King, but now they drifted apart, some in search of leftover delicacies from the women's dinner trays, others just wanting a quiet place to savor this rare night of freedom with their mistress absent.

"She would want Master Mordechai to know where she is," Darya said, and Parvaneh nodded. As one, they left the warmth of the women's quarters through the servants' door they used when they reported to Master Arman. But now, they turned their steps toward the main entrance, the *paradaisia* and the King's Gate. They remembered snaking through the gate in the bed of Kansbar's wagon when he had first brought them to work in the palace. They had been wide-eyed with wonder at the magnificence surrounding them. Now they were part of it—part of the invisible workforce that made it function.

They explained their errand to the soldiers guarding the inside of the gate, who were warming their hands over a small fire pit. The girls were permitted to pass through to the serpentine passageway lined with doorways. As always, Master Mordechai's young assistant opened his office door almost immediately when they knocked, and, as always, the girls lowered their eyes demurely when they saw him. He was a youth just a few years older than they were, with dark eyes and black curly hair beneath a Judean skullcap. When they had had a chance to ask Nasim about it, the old slave had explained that the cap was a reminder to the Judeans that their God was always above them.

Seeing the boy always made the girls feel shy and confused. Courteously, although smiling slightly at their discomfort, the assistant ushered them inside and asked them to wait while he knocked on the door to the inner room and entered. They heard him speak just a few quiet words before Master Mordechai appeared in the doorway. The dim light of the oil lamps muted the blue of his immaculate tunic and softened the contours of his skullcap and strange Judean beard.

"Ah, my young messengers," he greeted them with a smile. "Is everything well with my dear Lady Esther?"

"She is very well, sir," Parvaneh replied with a curtsy. "The Lady Esther is with the King."

"With the King!" the man repeated. He waved them

toward chairs and sat down himself while the youth leaned against the doorpost of the inner chamber. "She was summoned?" he asked, almost as though he were thinking out loud, rather than asking a question. "In spite of the fact that they know nothing about her?"

"Yes, sir," Darya replied. "Master Hegai escorted her to the King this evening. She has been preparing for three days."

"She looked very beautiful, sir," Parvaneh added.

"Like a queen, sir," Darya put in.

Mordechai smiled. "Like a queen," he echoed softly. "Who would have thought it would come this far? We shall see, shall we not?" He stroked his gray beard and stared at the lamplight.

The girls sat awkwardly, not knowing if they were dismissed. The man seemed to have forgotten them, lost in thought. But suddenly he roused himself and looked at them directly.

"You have been loyal messengers and I thank you," he said. He turned to his assistant. "David, there is a small pouch of coins in my desk. Please get it and give it to the girls."

When the youth returned with the pouch, he handed it to Parvaneh, who sat closest to the doorway. She took it without daring to raise her eyes to look at him. "For both of you to share," Mordechai said. "After tonight, who knows what will be? Thank you for all of your messages."

The girls murmured their thanks and rose to leave. But Darya stopped and turned back. "Sir. Please. Forgive me for asking. But why did we do this? Why were we sent here so often?"

She wasn't sure what sort of answer she was expecting, but Mordechai simply smiled and said, "The Lady Esther is a friend. I wanted to know that she was well."

"But..." Darya was certain there was more to it than that. She was sure this man was somehow connected to Esther's mysterious secretiveness. But she did not know how to phrase her questions, and she did not know if she really wanted answers.

"Come, Darya," Parvaneh said, taking her arm. "We must go back."

They left the office and began retracing their steps, but before they reached the guards at the inner gate, someone stepped from the shadows and blocked their path. It was Behrooz.

"Did you lose your way?" he mocked, his arms folded across his chest and his sinister smile stretching his lips. "Or does the Lady Esther now have an office in the King's Gate?"

"Please, sir. We must return to the women's quarters," Parvaneh said, taking a step toward him. But he did not move aside.

"What is your business with the Judean?" he demanded, the smile fading from his face. His question was greeted with silence and he said harshly, "Speak up. I want an answer."

"Please, sir," Parvaneh tried again. "We are expected in the women's quarters."

Behrooz grabbed her arm roughly. "And what I expect is an answer." He snatched the money pouch from her hand and demanded, "What is your business here?"

"Ow!" Parvaneh cried. "You are hurting me. Please."

"Let her go," Darya begged, stepping forward to try to free her friend from his grasp. Behrooz swung out at her, hitting her in the face with the money pouch and sending her sprawling backwards against the stone wall of the passageway. "Answer me!" he growled at Parvaneh.

"Leave them be!" came Mordechai's voice from behind the girls. "They are just children. Let them go."

"Ah, the Judean himself," Behrooz said, his sly smile returning. "And a Judean assistant," he added, as David appeared beside Mordechai. Slowly he loosened his grip on Parvaneh. "Why are these girls here? What is their business with you?"

Mordechai appraised Behrooz coolly. "Who are you, sir? Why all these questions? Why is my business your concern?"

Behrooz drew himself up. He was taller than Mordechai and he stared down at him. "I report to Master Arman. He would want to know why two of the Lady Esther's handmaidens were at the King's Gate closeted with a chief representative of the Judeans of the Empire." He shook the money pouch. "And what have they been paid for?"

"I see," Mordechai replied. "Tell your *master*"—he emphasized the word and Behrooz flinched—"tell him that he is welcome to visit me in my office any time to ask his questions. And now, sir, return the pouch, step aside, and let these girls pass, or I will call the guards."

Grudgingly, Behrooz did as he was told, but his glare made it evident that the Judean was now his enemy. Mordechai and David shepherded the girls through the passage to the inner gate. They all looked around, but Behrooz had disappeared.

"You had best accompany the girls to the women's quarters," Mordechai instructed David, "to make sure they arrive there safely." Then he bade them goodnight and turned back toward his office.

"Who was that man?" David asked the girls as they walked through the *paradaisia*.

"His name is Master Behrooz," Parvaneh replied, her eyes glued to the path. "More than that, we do not know—except that it is never good for us when he appears."

"Are you both all right?" David asked. "He was hurting you," he said to Parvaneh, but she just shrugged. "And you hit the wall hard," he added, peering at Darya.

"I will be fine," Darya murmured, pleased that he was concerned for her, but, like Parvaneh, not daring to look at him. Her shoulder ached where it had banged against the stone wall, and her cheek throbbed where the money pouch had hit it, yet David's attention was making her feel better.

"Be sure to tell us if he bothers you again," David told the girls when they reached the entrance to the women's quarters. "Master Mordechai is a good man with power and connections. He will help you."

As David raised his arm in farewell, Darya finally gathered enough courage to peek at him. Even in the dim light of the night-time gardens, she could see that he had the kind of smile that made her feel comforted and protected. She stood watching him disappear down the path until Parvaneh grabbed her arm and pulled her inside.

Eighteen

"This is my last night here—and maybe yours too," Darya whispered despondently to Parvaneh in the muted light of the women's courtyard. The girls were curled up on the floor beside the wall of the central fountain, their favorite sleeping place, with soft cushions beneath their heads. But with David gone, all Darya could picture was the menacing face of Behrooz, and all she could think of were his questions and suspicions, and what he would report to Master Arman. "Tomorrow—maybe even tonight—Master Arman will send for me and send me back to Golnar." Darya thought for a moment, then added, "And you—we can hope that if you must leave the women's quarters, he will let you work with your mother in the kitchens."

"We have done nothing," Parvaneh replied softly but urgently, trying to reassure herself as well as Darya. "We simply spoke to Master Mordechai. That is not treason."

"Perhaps it is not treason, but we did not report it to Master Arman. Lady Esther sent us regularly to the King's Gate and we never mentioned it. If Master Arman should find that out, he will not be pleased."

"Maybe Behrooz will say nothing," Parvaneh said hopefully, but both girls knew that would not be the case.

In fact, they were certain Behrooz had gone directly to Arman after the confrontation with Master Mordechai.

"What will become of us?" Parvaneh murmured, her voice catching. "You with Golnar ... and me ... perhaps I will be put out on the street alone. Who will hire me? How will I live?"

They lay tensely, listening to the music of the cascading water that had always been so peaceful and comforting. Now it seemed to mock them as a reminder of all they were about to lose.

"How did I ever think these quarters were like a prison?" Darya whispered. She peered through the soft night-time lamplight at the gilt and mosaics and marble that surrounded her. Then she mouthed silently, *Forgive me, dear* ahura, *for not appreciating all that you gave me.* But even as she prayed, she could not suppress her old feeling that the *ahura* would be deaf to her pleas, that she was not part of their Persian circle. Then she pictured Esther praying silently in her room and thought of her words—that she prayed to the creator of the world whose name did not matter.

Creator of the world. Darya turned the words over in her mind, examining them from all angles. The world included everything there was—all people, all animals, all lands, all seas, all rulers, all countries—so the creator of the world would have created everything and everybody, including Darya herself.

Suddenly Darya felt she understood something about gods and prayer that had never been clear to her before.

It did not matter if she was Persian or barbarian or Judean or from the lands far to the east. It did not matter if she was free or a slave. And it did not matter if she knew where she came from or who her family was or how she had become a slave. Her creator would be the same wherever she was from and whoever she was. She had the freedom to pray, and she had the freedom to hope for protection.

Darya let out her breath and relaxed. "It will be all right," she whispered to Parvaneh.

"How do you know? What will we say to Master Arman?"

"We will tell him the truth—that we did not think the visits were important because we never said anything more than that the Lady Esther was well."

"He will say that we were not supposed to judge for ourselves what was important," Parvaneh insisted. "And he will say that we did not tell him because we wanted to protect our lady."

"I suppose … he would be correct," Darya agreed haltingly. "But poor judgment is not a crime," she said more loudly and firmly. She raised her head, remembering Lady Esther saying the same thing about her secrecy. "And neither is trying to protect our lady." She yawned and lay back down, shifting into a more comfortable position against the fountain. "Let us sleep. If this *is* our last night in the women's quarters, let us enjoy it."

Parvaneh peered at her in the dim light. "You sound different," she murmured.

"In what way?"

"I am not sure. Just not like Darya."

Darya thought about that as she drifted off to sleep. She sounded different, and she felt different too. The women's quarters had changed her, especially working for Lady Esther.

∞

It was still dark when Arman sent for them. Hegai shook them awake gently but insistently and quietly told them to follow him out of the women's quarters. He gazed at them sadly as he handed them over to two palace guards, who marched them grimly through the cold night to the storehouse, where Behrooz and his self-satisfied smirk sat with Master Arman in his office.

Darya's newfound confidence deserted her as she stood quaking with Parvaneh before Master Arman's desk. The interrogation was quick and precise, and none of the girls' planned defenses withstood the assault. No, they were not accused of treason, but they had made themselves useless to Master Arman, and as such, had no purpose in the women's quarters. Darya would be remanded to Golnar immediately. Parvaneh, as a free-born girl, could leave the palace grounds, if she wished—leave them with no place to go and a black mark against her—but if she chose to stay, she would also be ruled by Golnar. Terrified and confused, Parvaneh mumbled that she would stay with Darya.

In shock, the girls marched woodenly between the guards to the female slave barracks, where Golnar and her rod were awakened to receive them.

"I knew you'd be back!" the flame-haired woman exclaimed almost gleefully to Darya. "And with your plotting friend too." She prodded them roughly into a dark corner of the barracks that smelled of garbage and urine. "Not a word from either one of you until morning," she warned, "unless you want a beating like the one you remember."

The two girls sat close together, shivering, their backs to the wall, their eyes fearful, waiting silently for the first glimmer of dawn and the life of horror that Darya remembered so well.

Nineteen

For Darya, it was awful to be back in the chamber-pot shed in the morning, but for Parvaneh, it was almost unbearable. Darya watched with concern as her friend gagged repeatedly each time she lifted a pot filled with night soil and emptied it into the long trough.

"Take off your sash and wrap it around your nose and mouth," Darya suggested. "It will lessen the smell."

Parvaneh nodded and clumsily tried to untie the sash around her waist. But her fingers were shaking too much and she couldn't see clearly because her eyes were swimming with tears. Darya stooped before her, gently pushed the other girl's hands away, and untied the cloth. Then she wrapped it carefully around Parvaneh's face, all the while glancing over her shoulder to make sure Golnar was not entering the shed to check that they were working. Both girls already had bruises on their backs from the prods and pokes of the head slave's rod, starting at first light, before finally being ordered into the shed. Almost happily, Golnar had warned them that she would be checking on them throughout the day and that they would pay dearly for anything that looked like slacking.

"Thank you," Parvaneh murmured to Darya, her voice muffled by the cloth. She wiped away her tears with her sleeve and stooped to pick up another pot. Darya watched her worriedly for a moment before returning to her own work. She did not know how Parvaneh would survive this. The girl had always worked beside her mother in the kitchen, and she had always been efficient and willing in the women's quarters, but the rod and the shed—they were not what she was used to. She pictured Jaleh hugging Parvaneh on her twelfth birthday, and the girl flitting about like a butterfly in her gossamer shawl. It seemed like ages ago—in another life. There would be no hugs or gifts under Golnar.

But Darya was wrong. It was not until late afternoon of that long, dreadful day—not until Golnar had entered the shed three times, always finding a reason to wield the rod, and not until the girls were faint with hunger because Golnar had made sure almost nothing was left in the bottom of the pots when she finally allowed them a break for the midday meal—but Jaleh did come to the shed. Parvaneh set down the pot she was scrubbing in boiling water and ran to her mother, who enfolded her in her arms.

"My poor child," Jaleh murmured. "How did this happen? What have you girls done?" Her glance took in Darya as well. "Nasim and I were summoned to Master Arman's office. He asked us strange questions about the King's Gate and secret messages, but neither of us had any idea what it was all about. We were both so confused that Master Arman realized we knew nothing. He told us to return to our work, but warned us that any missteps would put me on the street and Nasim in the poorhouse." She looked at Darya again, then pushed Parvaneh's sash down so she could see her daughter's face, which had been buried against her chest as she hugged her. Sadly, she stroked a purple bruise on Parvaneh's cheek. "What have you girls done?" she repeated softly.

Neither girl could meet Jaleh's eyes, and Parvaneh burrowed her face into her mother's chest again. Darya was horrified to realize that her actions could have hurt Jaleh and Nasim. How had she ever thought she could keep anything from Master Arman? He had eyes and ears everywhere. She knew that. She had been so stupid.

"We were trying to protect the Lady Esther," Darya said lamely, thinking how silly it sounded—a slave girl and a servant, believing they had some sort of power. "But Master Behrooz saw us—"

"Behrooz!" Jaleh burst out. "What does that dog have to do with this?"

"He reports to Master Arman," Darya said. "He saw us leaving Master Mordechai's office in the King's Gate, and he—"

"Who is this Master Mordechai? And what business did you have in the King's Gate?" Jaleh shook her head and repeated a third time, "What have you girls done?"

Hanging her head, Darya tried to explain as best she could how they had carried messages, time after time, from Lady Esther to her friend Master Mordechai. "But it was only to say that she was well," Darya insisted. "Always the same and nothing more. And Master Arman is so suspicious of her. We were afraid that if we said anything at all, it would not go well for her."

Parvaneh raised her tear-streaked face. "We wanted only to help her," she said softly.

Jaleh was silent for a moment, gently smoothing her daughter's tangled hair. "Let us hope she knows that and remembers you," she said. "Because *she* is the one who can be of help to *you*—now that she will be Queen."

"Queen!" both girls exclaimed. For a moment, they forgot their predicament and their faces lit up with joy.

"She was so beautiful when she went to the King," Parvaneh breathed. "It seems so long ago. Was it only last night?"

"It was proclaimed at noon today," Jaleh told them. "In the palace, in the square, all over the city, and I suppose the news is being spread all over the Empire as we speak. The Lady Esther will be the new Queen in Susa." She smiled at the girls' happiness for their lady. "There will be dinners and parties and a coronation. It will be a busy time in this palace."

Parvaneh's face fell. "Perhaps too busy for Lady Esther to think about us," she murmured.

"She is not like that!" Darya exclaimed. For a moment, her hand went to the scar on her neck that still remained from the years of the slave collar chafing her—the collar that Esther had ordered removed. "She cares about people. She remembers them, and she once told me that if I was being threatened, she would help me if she could."

"She can only try to help if she knows about it," Parvaneh retorted. "How will she know what happened to us?"

"We will not be there to serve her on the sixth and seventh days," Darya pointed out. "She will notice. You know she will."

"Not if all of her handmaidens are replaced now that she will be Queen," Parvaneh responded in despair. "Maybe we were only her handmaidens for the women's quarters." She burrowed her face against her mother once more.

"Hush," Jaleh soothed her, stroking her hair again. "There must be a way for us to get word to her." They were all silent for a moment. "What of her friend in the King's Gate?" Jaleh asked. "I have no way to speak to the future Queen, but perhaps I can get word to her through her friend."

"Master Mordechai," Parvaneh told her. "Yes, *Ema*, please try," she added desperately. "I cannot bear it here any longer!"

"Just one day, and you cannot bear it?" Golnar taunted as she entered the shed. "Let us see just how much you cannot bear," she sneered, raising her rod and approaching Parvaneh.

Golnar was powerful and a full head taller than Jaleh, but the chief slave was not expecting any opposition. In one swift movement, Jaleh pushed Parvaneh behind her and grabbed the rod out of Golnar's hand. "Do not dare!" she seethed at Golnar. "Do not touch these girls again!" She had never set eyes on Golnar before, but she had no doubt that this was the woman who had beaten Darya so brutally and had put today's bruises on the girls.

Golnar was speechless for a moment, then she laughed harshly. "Who are you to stop me, woman? I am Golnar. I work for Master Arman, and I order you out of this shed."

Jaleh stood her ground. "You order me? You are a slave!" she exclaimed. "I am Jaleh—mother of Parvaneh and protector of Darya. I also work for Master Arman—as well as for the King and the new Queen. And I will make sure to have you thrown off the palace grounds and set to work in a dung heap if you ever hurt these girls again!"

Golnar had no way of knowing how much power Jaleh really had, but it was obvious that the cook's authoritative manner gave her pause. "These girls should be working," she said almost apologetically.

"And so should you," Jaleh retorted. She used Golnar's own rod to prod the giant slave out the doorway of the shed, then she turned to face the two astonished girls. "I will go to the King's Gate as soon as I can," she assured them. "Oh—and I brought these for you." From her sash, she untied a small sack filled with soft rolls and handed it to the girls. "I assumed you probably were not getting enough to eat."

Twenty

The rolls were long gone by the next afternoon, and Jaleh's appearance in the shed the day before began to feel like a dream. Golnar found herself another rod, although she did not use it as freely—at least not on the girls. Instead, she made sure they had even less to eat than previously. Only a visit to the shed by Nasim raised the girls' spirits. But he was filled with worrisome talk of the new Queen.

"People are saying she was sent here by the *daeva*," he told them in a low voice, looking over his shoulder to make sure he was not overheard. "They say that she has dark powers."

"Why would they say that?" Darya asked in surprise, also keeping her voice low.

"Why else was she chosen? And so quickly!" Nasim retorted. "The King was with her just one night. She is completely unknown. She will say nothing about her home, her family, her people. And yet the King insists he must have her as his Queen. She is a witch. That is what people are saying."

"She is no such thing!" Parvaneh exclaimed.

"Hush!" Nasim warned. "The walls have ears, and we are talking about the new Queen."

"She is no such thing," Parvaneh repeated much more quietly. "She is lovely and kind and good. That is what the King saw in just one night. And that is what the people will see when they have the chance."

"Perhaps she does have some sort of power," Darya put in, thinking of how Hegai had favored Esther, and how all her handmaidens adored her. "But it is the power of the *ahura*, not the *daeva*. Parvaneh is right. That is what the King saw."

Nasim just shook his head as he moved toward the doorway to return to the stables. "Whatever power she has, it will need to be strong," he said, almost whispering, "because there are many who are not pleased with this choice."

The girls looked at each other with concern when he left. "She could be in danger," Darya murmured.

Parvaneh nodded. "And if she is in danger, then there is little hope she will be able to help us."

Darya wanted so much to contradict her friend, but she realized that Parvaneh was right. "We cannot help her, and we cannot help ourselves," she said. Wearily, she lifted a chamber pot and dipped it in the cauldron of boiling water, trying her best not to scald her fingers as she had already done countless times in the past two days.

The girls worked silently until nightfall. They loaded the cleaned pots onto carts for other slaves to wheel back to the palace and place discreetly in each bedroom. Hopelessly, they dragged themselves back to the slave quarters, where they scraped another meager meal from the bottom of the pots, then crawled into their cold, dark corner, trying their best not to be noticed by Golnar.

The dawn brought the rising winter sun, but no lifting of their spirits. It seemed that Jaleh had not been able to help them. Perhaps she had never been able to speak to Master Mordechai. Or perhaps she had, and Mordechai had not been able to speak to the Lady Esther. Or perhaps he had, and Esther was too involved in dealing with all her newfound enemies to be able to turn her attention to the troubles of her former handmaidens.

Golnar was in a fouler mood than usual, and using her rod freely again. The girls entered the malodorous shed massaging new bruises on their shoulders. But they did not speak to each other or even look at each other, almost as if they did not want to give voice to what was on their minds—that this was their life now—day after day, this was where they would be. No more women's quarters, or fountains, or fancy foods. No more kind words, or letter-writing, or trinkets.

Darya thought of the coins she had been saving, hoping to buy her freedom someday. She had given them to the Lady Esther for safekeeping. Who knew where they were now? Who knew if she would ever see them again? After living differently in the women's quarters, Darya found her slavery difficult to bear. She had been concerned about Parvaneh working in the shed, but she realized that she herself was having trouble as well.

Both girls were bent over the trough and so immersed in

their own gloomy thoughts that neither of them was aware
that somebody else had entered the shed. They wheeled
around when they heard someone clear his throat and say,
"Pardon me," in a quiet, courteous voice.

"David!" Darya breathed. She stared at him in his fine,
spotless clothing, trying to make sense of his unexpected
appearance in the shed. She watched him cover his nose
and mouth with his hand and take a step backward toward
the doorway where there was some fresher air. And instead
of the shyness she had always felt around him, she felt
something different and painful: shame. She was ashamed
to be working in the shed, ashamed to be dirty and smelly
and disheveled, but most of all, ashamed to be what she
was—a slave. He had never seen her this way. He only
knew her as Lady Esther's handmaiden, as the scribe of the
women's quarters, washed and brushed and presentable.
She wanted to shrivel up and sink into the ground.

Parvaneh stared at David as well, half her face concealed
by her sash, but then she lowered her eyes, apparently as
embarrassed before him as Darya was.

David cleared his throat again and, after studying what
he could see of their expressions, deliberately lowered his
hand from his face. It was as if he were trying to assure
the girls that they and their surroundings did not disgust
him. "Master Mordechai sent me as soon as he received
word from the future Queen," he explained, his tone the
same as it had always been with them. "He asked me to
extend his apologies that it took so long from the time

Madame Jaleh came to him until he could send a message to Lady Esther and receive one in return. But the palace is preparing frantically for the wedding and coronation, and guards are everywhere, protecting the King and the future Queen. It was no simple matter."

Slowly, Parvaneh raised her eyes and lowered the sash from her face. "Lady Esther knows where we are?" she asked, a touch of hope in her voice.

David nodded. "She finally received Master Mordechai's message."

"And she sent a message in return?" Darya asked, as afraid to hope as Parvaneh.

"Yes," David replied. "As soon as Master Mordechai received word from her, he sent me to tell you."

"Please," Darya almost begged in a small voice. "What was her message?"

"Why, for both of you to return to the palace, of course!" David exclaimed, laughing. "I thought you understood that. Master Arman will be sending for you, but Master Mordechai wanted you to hear the news as soon as possible."

He was astonished when both girls began to smile at the news, then clung to each other and broke down in tears.

Twenty-One
Five Years Later

Darya sat on velvety grass in the mini-paradise of the Queen's garden, a papyrus scroll spread open on her lap. It was filled from top to bottom with Monir's carefully crafted letters and words, and there was just enough light remaining in the evening sky of early spring to read it. The letter made Darya smile.

"She is well?" Parvaneh asked, from her perch on the low stone wall against which Darya leaned.

"More than well," Darya replied. "She has learned to stand up for herself. A few months ago, she demanded that she be allowed to use some of her money to hire a tutor so that she could improve her reading and writing, and her uncle forced her aunt to agree. Just look at this scroll." Darya held it up for Parvaneh to see. "The lettering is so much better. And she sounds so happy. She has new friends in Persepolis, and she traveled around the city with them. They wanted to see how the palace and all the King's other new building projects were coming along."

"Have you finished reading it?" Parvaneh asked. "I would like to see what else she wrote."

"Shall we read it together?" Darya asked, handing her the scroll, but Parvaneh shook her head.

"Let me try on my own. You have taught me well, and I think I can get through it."

Darya watched with satisfaction as Parvaneh moved her lips silently while reading the scroll. The Queen had asked Darya to use some of her free time to teach the other handmaidens to read, but Parvaneh had been her only avid pupil.

"All those little shapes on the papyrus make my head ache," one of the handmaidens had complained, and several others agreed. "Why does the Queen want us to do this?" she had whined. "It will not make us serve her any better."

"But it will," Darya had insisted. "The more of us who know how to read, the more we can protect our Queen if anyone is trying to harm her."

"The palace guard is here to protect her," the handmaiden had countered, "and you and Parvaneh can do the reading if that is needed."

Darya had shrugged her shoulders helplessly and doubled her efforts to teach Parvaneh. Now here she was, reading Monir's letter on her own.

"She wants to know more about Crown Prince Artaxerxes." Parvaneh laughed and looked at Darya. "You told her that sometimes we are allowed to play with him in the royal nursery?"

Darya nodded. "I knew she would enjoy hearing about him—how cute he is, and that he has Queen Esther's sweetness."

"Did you read about Monir's new friend Leah?" Parvaneh asked, looking up again from the letter. Darya nodded a second time, and Parvaneh continued, "I am not sure I understand what Monir wrote about her. I think she said that Leah is a Judean."

"She is," Darya affirmed. "The daughter of a merchant who only recently started doing business with Monir's uncle."

"What does she say after that?" Parvaneh asked. "Something about how Leah looks."

Darya laughed. "She says that Leah reminds her of me—how she remembers me back when I was twelve. But remember, she has not seen me in five years, and of course I have changed! Yet the resemblance made her want to become friends with this girl in the first place."

Parvaneh smiled and turned back to the letter. "What is this?" she exclaimed. "Did she write that her aunt and uncle are beginning to look for suitors for her?"

"It seems that way," Darya said. "After all, she is fifteen years old—marriageable age."

"I suppose so," Parvaneh replied, laying the letter in her lap. "You and I are two years older than that, and it worries me."

"How so?"

"Because other people will choose who we marry!" Parvaneh burst out. "And it might not be someone we want." She looked at Darya with a troubled expression. "What if I am forced to marry someone awful like Behrooz!"

Darya stood and leaned against the stone wall where Parvaneh sat. Gently, she patted Parvaneh's arm. "Your mother would never let that happen," she soothed. "You know that. When the time is right, she will talk to Master Arman and find you a respectable match." She smiled mischievously. "Maybe even someone handsome and young—like that new soldier at the King's Gate who always seems to have something to say to you."

Parvaneh's face reddened. "He just wishes me a good day or asks if I need an escort for my errand. Majeed only wants to be sure I am safe."

Darya laughed. "Majeed, is it? You already know his name?"

Parvaneh playfully smacked Darya's hand. "Yes, I know his name. He is nice to me. He looks out for me." Her face clouded. "Not like Behrooz. All my life, whenever he appeared, he always seemed to have some kind of evil plans. You were there too, so you know this. What if he has plans about whom I should marry?"

Darya stared at her. "I do not understand," she said in confusion. "Why do you keep thinking that Master Behrooz could have something to do with a suitor for you?"

"Because all these years, it has always seemed as though Behrooz has some sort of power over my mother," Parvaneh answered tensely. "You have seen it. The way he has always shown up somewhere near her, like here in the palace, even though she makes it very clear she does not want him around. The way he somehow pushes her to do things she does not want to do."

Darya did not know what to say, and Parvaneh continued, "Behrooz works for Master Arman. He is close with him. I am afraid that if he wants something…"

"Your mother also works for Master Arman," Darya countered. "He respects her. He will listen to her and make sure you have the proper match and that Master Behrooz has nothing to do with it."

"I hope you are right," Parvaneh said. She took a shaky breath and looked up at the darkening sky. Then she turned to her friend and forced a smile. "Perhaps there will be a handsome young suitor for you too."

Darya shook her head. "I am a slave, Parvaneh. I am lucky to work for the Queen, but I am still a slave. I do not believe there are any suitors in my future."

"What about the coins and trinkets you saved?" Parvaneh asked. "You used to talk about buying your freedom. Why not ask the Queen about it? Ask her how much more you need, and whether there is a way for you to do it."

Darya was silent and Parvaneh could hardly see her expression in the dusk. "I am not sure I still want freedom," Darya finally said quietly. "What would I do with it? I have no one outside these walls. If I left here, what would I do? Where would I go? The people I care about are here—you, your mother, the Queen, Nasim…."

"And David," Parvaneh finished for her. It was her turn to laugh. "If you left here, you would no longer see him every time he has a reason to come to the Queen's quarters."

Darya was grateful for the gathering darkness so that

Parvaneh could not see her blush. "He comes here with messages from Master Mordechai," she said defensively. "He delivers them to you as well as to me."

Parvaneh laughed again. "Yes, he sometimes delivers them to me, but he always seems more pleased to deliver them to you." She grabbed Darya's arm. "I think he is smitten with you, Darya. And if you were free...."

Darya's heart pounded, but she shook her head slowly. She pictured David in his fine clothing, working in the King's Gate. "He works for Master Mordechai," she whispered. "He comes from a well-to-do family who were all lost to the plague, and now he is Master Mordechai's ward. And he is a Judean, devoted to his religion and its laws. He is always courteous to me, but more than that?" She shook her head again. "Master Mordechai will find him a high-born Judean girl to marry—someone educated and beautiful and..." Darya's voice caught in her throat and she blinked back tears.

Parvaneh squeezed her arm. "You cannot be sure of that," she insisted. "You could learn about his religion and its laws. You could even become a Judean yourself, as some Persians already have." Darya was still shaking her head despondently, and Parvaneh said encouragingly, "You should talk to the Queen about it. You know you are her favorite, and you know she has the power to make things happen."

Darya sighed. "You and I both know that the Queen has more important concerns than my freedom. She still keeps her secrets, and there are those that do not trust her, even after she has been Queen for five years. And she is concerned for the King. There are those who still grumble about losing the war in Greece, and about the high taxes that have been levied to pay for that and for all the building projects." She shivered. "I am sure there are others out there like those two courtiers that Master Mordechai caught right after Lady Esther became Queen. Do you remember?"

Parvaneh shivered as well. "How could I ever forget? They plotted against the King. What were their names again? Bigthan and … and…?"

"Teresh," Darya filled in. "But they made the mistake of talking about their plans near the King's Gate, and Master Mordechai overheard them. Remember? He reported it to the Queen, and they were hanged before they could do any harm. But there could be others."

"I know," Parvaneh agreed. "All those expensive building projects Monir wrote about only make things worse. Perhaps the new Chief Minister, Haman, will know how to make the problems go away. The King seems to think so."

Darya was silent for a few moments, then whispered, "Master Haman frightens me."

"He frightens me, too," Parvaneh agreed. "The way he is never seen alone. The way he marches around the palace with all those followers."

"With Behrooz and others like him," Darya put in, "like a small private army. I have heard rumors that he has followers in other cities besides Susa."

Parvaneh shuddered at Behrooz's name. "Even so," she insisted, "he might have all those followers because he is powerful and knows how to get things done. Maybe that is why the King made him Chief Minister. Maybe it will be good for the King and our Queen."

"I hope so," Darya murmured, pushing herself upright away from the wall. "But David is not one of his admirers, and neither is Master Mordechai. David has told me they do not trust him. They think he is more interested in his own power than the King's. In fact, David told me that Master Mordechai refuses to bow when Master Haman passes by, and that the minister is furious."

"How does Master Mordechai dare?" Parvaneh wondered. "Haman is Chief Minister. Is it not dangerous to refuse to bow to him?"

"I am sure it is," Darya replied. "But Master Mordechai has power too. He is a chief Judean official and their representative to the King. And everyone knows he is a favorite of the Queen. It might be dangerous for Master Mordechai not to bow, but it might also be dangerous for Master Haman to try to do anything about it."

The girls did not speak further as they slowly returned to their work in the Queen's chambers, but Darya kept thinking about their conversation. She had insisted to Parvaneh that the Queen had more important concerns on her mind, but she could not help wondering if perhaps she should talk to the Queen about her freedom. And if she were free, she could not help wondering if perhaps that might make David and Master Mordechai see her in a different light.

Twenty-Two

By the next morning, Darya had gathered the courage to approach Queen Esther about her freedom, and possibly even about David. She was walking toward the Queen's chambers when she saw Hasach, the Queen's favorite guard, hurry into the chambers ahead of her.

"I do not understand," the Queen was exclaiming, as Darya reached the entrance to the apartment. "Master Mordechai is wearing sackcloth? He is sitting in the square before the palace wearing sackcloth?"

"Yes, Your Highness," Hasach replied. "I saw him as I was returning from an errand in the square. And he is not alone. There are other Judeans sitting there with him, right in the middle of the square, as though they want to be sure everyone notices them. I knew you would want to be informed."

The Queen paced the room in agitation. "I do not understand!" she kept repeating. "Why would he do this?" She looked up and saw Darya in the doorway. "Darya! Good! I am glad you are here. Run to the storeroom for some clean clothing for Master Mordechai, then go out to the square with Hasach. Find out what is going on and report back to me immediately!"

Darya ran. She had never seen the Queen so agitated, and she could not imagine Master Mordechai wearing sackcloth. She pictured him in his immaculate tunic and trousers and could think of him no other way. But when she and Hasach exited the King's Gate, there he was, sitting on the ground in sackcloth. His face was smeared with ashes. He was rocking back and forth, and seemed to be praying. Darya glanced around and saw other Judeans on the ground close by, doing the same. She gasped when she noticed that one of them was David. Other people in the square clustered in small groups, pointing and murmuring. A few that Darya recognized as members of Haman's inner circle had triumphant expressions on their faces.

Darya's first instinct was to rush to David, to beg him to explain to her what was happening, to have him look at her like the David she knew. But when he glanced her way, even though he nodded his head slightly in greeting, he seemed so distant from her, so separate. She shuddered and hesitantly approached Master Mordechai instead. She crouched before him; Hasach stood close behind her.

"Sir," Darya said softly, and waited for Mordechai to stop rocking and look at her. "The Queen has sent you clean clothing." She held it out to him. "Her Majesty is concerned for you and wishes to know what this is all about."

Even though he was facing her, it took a few moments for Mordechai's eyes to fully focus on her. His attention seemed to be on something far distant, and it took him some effort to concentrate on her words.

"Darya," he murmured, "and Hasach. Good. I knew you would come. I knew that if we sat here in the square she would send you."

"The Queen is concerned, sir," Hasach said, holding out his hand. "Let me help you up. We will go to your office and I will help you change your clothing."

Mordechai stared at the outstretched hand as though it were some foreign object. He made no move to rise. "Tell the Queen," he began slowly, searching for the right words. "Tell the Queen that ... that my people are in danger."

"Your people?" Darya questioned. "The Judeans? How so? Your people have the same protections as any others in the Empire. Why, you, sir"—she flung out her arm and pointed toward the palace—"you have your office right there, in the King's Gate! How can you be in danger?"

"So I thought," Mordechai said quietly. "Until now. Until I saw this." He held up a papyrus scroll that had been lying on the ground next to him. Hasach just stared at it, but Darya unrolled it and read through its contents in growing horror.

"What does it say?" Hasach asked, peering over her shoulder, even though he could not read it. "Is that the King's seal?"

"Yes," she responded in a choked voice, struggling to form the words. "It has the seal, and it says that the Judeans ... the Judeans ... are marked for death...."

Hasach was dumbstruck. "Death?" he finally whispered. "Death? I do not understand."

"Death," Darya repeated. She looked back at the scroll, as if to be sure she had read it right. "They are marked for death ... on a set day at the end of the year." Her voice dropped to a whisper as she lay the scroll back down on the ground. "All of them—men, women, and even children—throughout the Empire, and their property will be taken."

Hasach stared at the scroll. "But why? What have they done? That is not the Persian way," he protested. "That is not the way the Empire is ruled."

"It is not the way the Empire *was* ruled," Mordechai corrected him bitterly. "Until now."

"How could this happen?" Hasach asked in confusion. "What has changed?"

"We have a new Chief Minister," Mordechai spat out. "One who has been gathering an army of followers in Susa and in other cities throughout the Empire—followers who believe that it is not good for Persia to have so many foreigners living here. They believe that foreigners can hurt the Empire, that they steal jobs from the true Persians."

"But...." Hasach began incredulously, trying to gather his thoughts. "But Persia is filled with foreigners! The King has always said that all the different people that make up the Empire are the reason it is so strong."

Mordechai shook his head sadly. "All that has changed," he murmured. "Our new Chief Minister has the King's ear. He has convinced the King that because some people have different beliefs they are not loyal to the Empire, that some people are not worthy of his protection, and that it is better for the Empire for some people to be wiped off the face of the Earth so that their property will fill the King's treasury and pay for his wars and his building projects!"

Mordechai's voice had grown louder and more bitter as he spoke, but now it dropped so low that Hasach and Darya had to lean closer to hear him. "The Queen must plead for us. You must tell her that. Here"—he thrust the papyrus into Hasach's hand—"show her the scroll. She must go to the King and plead our case. She is our only hope."

Twenty-Three

"Plead for them?" Esther echoed, when Darya and Hasach had delivered Mordechai's message and the scroll. "How am I to do that?" She paced her chamber in agitation, the scroll clutched in her hand. "No one is permitted to enter the King's presence without being summoned, and I have not been summoned for at least thirty days. Why, just last week, I was told that a top advisor made the grave mistake of barging into the King's audience hall unannounced." She stopped pacing abruptly and faced Hasach. "Did you not hear about that?" she asked.

He nodded and murmured, "He disappeared, Majesty. No one knows what became of him."

"Precisely," the Queen continued. "If I simply appear before the King, he will become enraged, as he so often does. I might disappear like that advisor. Or I might suffer Queen Vashti's fate and be banished. I might even be condemned to death! What good would that do the Judeans?"

"Your Majesty is the King's favorite," Hasach reassured her. "He would never harm the Queen."

Esther's lips curled into a bitter smile. "The King's favorite," she repeated. "Queen Vashti also thought she was a favorite, and she had a great deal more power than

I have. Remember, she was the granddaughter of King Nebuchadnezzar of Babylon. Who am I?" She shook her head. "I am no longer a favorite. I am simply the mother of an heir to the throne, and the head wife in a court filled with beautiful women. You must tell Master Mordechai that I cannot help him."

But when Darya and Hasach made their way out to the square again to deliver the Queen's message, they were taken aback by Mordechai's reaction.

"The Queen refused to help?" he demanded, a fiery expression in his eyes. "What can she be thinking? Has she forgotten? Does she not realize…." His words trailed off, and he twisted around to stare at the palace gates in anger. But his anger subsided almost as quickly as it had flared up and was replaced by icy calm. "Darya," he said quietly. "Run to my office and bring me papyrus, quill, and ink. I would send David, but he would not be allowed through the gates in sackcloth."

He handed her the keys to his office, and she ran to do as he asked. The office was more than familiar to her because of all the years of carrying messages between Mordechai and the Queen, but she had never been there alone. It felt awkward to rummage through his things to find what he had requested, as though she were uncovering what ought to remain concealed. She was about to leave and lock the door, when she spied a small footstool. She grabbed it and returned to the square, where she placed everything before Mordechai.

He smiled as he watched her arrange the writing implements on the footstool, as though it were a small desk. "The Queen has said more than once that she can count on you to know what is needed without being told," he said appreciatively. "She thinks of you as so much more than a slave ... as do I."

He leaned forward, took up the quill and began composing his message, while Darya and Hasach turned away to afford him some privacy. Darya looked toward David, still sitting on the ground nearby, immersed in prayer. She wondered if he prayed to his Judean God the same way that she used to hear Jaleh pray to *Ahura Mazda*, or the same way that she often saw the Queen praying. She wished she knew more about the Judeans and their beliefs, as Parvaneh had suggested during their talk in the Queen's garden, and wondered why she had never asked David to tell her about them. Now it might be too late. David and his people were in mortal danger.

It seemed eons ago that she had decided to talk to the Queen about her freedom and about David. That was all shunted aside now, in spite of what Master Mordechai had said about how he and the Queen thought of her. She would not bring it up anymore, not with a sword hanging over David and his people—and not with them rallying together and making her feel shut out and separate. She glanced back at Mordechai and saw that he had completed his message.

"I have no sealing wax," he said, as he rolled the papyrus and handed it to Hasach. "But I trust that you will make sure that this is read only by the Queen."

"You have my word, sir," Hasach said, bowing. He helped Darya collect the implements, and the two of them returned to the palace.

∞

Queen Esther's face turned deathly pale when she read the new scroll. She rerolled it tightly, walked to the window of her chamber, leaned her head against it, and closed her eyes. She remained that way for so long that Darya and Hasach wondered if they should quietly take their leave. But just as they began to move toward the door, Esther began to speak. If her voice had had a color, it would have been the same chalk white as her face.

"Go to the square one more time and tell Master Mordechai that I will do as he asks," she said. "I will go before the King in three days' time, after I have prayed and fasted and prepared myself. I ask that Master Mordechai and all the people with him in the square pray and fast as well. And I ask that all my servants and handmaidens do the same. Perhaps I will succeed, perhaps not. But I will try."

Esther's demeanor made Darya shiver and gasp for breath, as though icy fingers encircled her neck where her slave collar had once been. She realized that, until this moment, she had agreed with Hasach that Esther was the King's favorite and that he would never harm her. Now she was no longer certain of that. After all, as Esther had pointed out, the King rarely requested her company anymore, in spite of the fact that she had borne him a son, and Queen Vashti had also once been a favorite.

Darya wanted desperately to pray for her Queen, as she had been asked. But her old doubts plagued her, as they always did. Who was she, and to whom should she pray? The Persian gods? The Judean God? Would anyone answer her prayers? Then, once again, she remembered Esther's words from years ago, the words that had comforted her that night when she and Parvaneh waited to be summoned before Master Arman—that she prayed to the creator of the world, whose name did not matter.

This night, Darya stood alone in the Queen's garden. She thought about the woman she served, who never made her feel like a slave, who always made her feel valued and cared for. Darya thought about what her life might have been like if she had never had the opportunity to serve the Queen, and what her life might be like if she could no longer serve the Queen. She thought about the Judeans in sackcloth and ashes in the square, and Mordechai's scroll, and Esther's deathly pale face. She thought about foreigners and outsiders, about free people and slaves, and about those deemed worthy of protection and those condemned to live life precariously. She gazed up at the star-filled sky and her lips moved silently in prayer.

Twenty-Four

Three nights later, Darya, Parvaneh, and Hasach stood in the shadows of the Queen's dining chamber, ready to do her bidding if anything was needed beyond the sumptuous banquet the kitchen staff was serving. In the shadows across the room from them stood Charbonah, one of the King's personal servants, along with half a dozen palace guards, who were always nearby when the King was present. After the three days of fasting and praying, everything had happened so quickly that Darya still could hardly believe the scene before her, illuminated by hundreds of candles in ornate golden lamps.

There was the Queen in all her beauty, reclining on her cushioned couch, with the King on another couch on one side and Chief Minister Haman on the other. A musician plucked soft music from the strings of a lyre, young boys slowly waved peacock-feather fans to freshen the air, and serving girls kept jeweled wine cups filled and golden trays brimming with every imaginable delicacy.

Was it only that morning that Esther had stood trembling at the entrance to the King's grand audience chamber, with Darya and Parvaneh attending her? She had followed Darya's suggestion to wear the gown she had selected for that first night when she had enchanted the King and he had chosen her as Queen. But nobody knew if that would be enough to gain his favor, if he would permit her to enter, or if he would angrily summon his guards to haul her off to banishment or death. Everyone knew about his violent temper. Everyone remembered Queen Vashti, and the advisor who was still missing. Everyone knew that the King often acted on impulse, although he usually regretted it later.

The images of what had happened next spooled through Darya's mind as she stood now in the dining hall: how the King noticed Esther in the entryway; how he extended his golden scepter toward her and bade her approach; how she touched its tip with trepidation and bowed before him; and, finally, how he gently asked her what was troubling her and assured her that he would gladly give her half the kingdom if she requested it!

Darya and Parvaneh had stared at each other in joy and disbelief while they waited to hear how Esther would respond to the King's warmth and generosity. He was prepared to give her almost anything, but would that include the lives and the safety of a large group of his subjects? Would that include accepting the loss of a great deal of property that he desperately needed for his treasury? Clearly, the Queen was not ready to find that out yet because all she asked was that the King and his Chief Minister honor her with their presence at a feast that evening.

And so here they were, the King smiling at Esther like he had when they were first married, and Haman basking in the knowledge that he was the only courtier who had been invited to this intimate royal dinner. The men ate and drank, talked and drank, laughed and drank, while the Queen smiled at them graciously and sipped delicately from her cup, which Darya noticed had never been refilled.

"The King and the Minister are getting drunk," Darya whispered to her companions. "Is that what the Queen wants? She has not yet made her request."

"It is the Persian way," Hasach explained softly. "No business will be done before all the eating, and especially the drinking, are completed. Sometimes, nothing at all will get done at a banquet, and there will have to be a second one for any business."

Sure enough, when the King finally turned to Esther and, his words slurring, asked what wishes he could grant for her, she smiled sweetly and requested that he and the Minister return the following evening for a second feast.

∞

"All that again tomorrow," Parvaneh complained later that night, as she and Darya rolled out their sleeping mats in a corner of an anteroom of the Queen's apartments. "Nothing accomplished. The Judeans still in danger. Just eating and drinking and drinking and drinking…."

Darya laughed softly, careful not to disturb the Queen, who was falling asleep in the adjoining room. "It is like Hasach explained. Business will be done tomorrow night. The Queen wants the King in the best mood possible when she makes her request. She is only trying to help Master Mordechai and his people."

But in spite of her own reassuring words, Darya tossed uncomfortably on her mat and could not settle down. She heard Parvaneh breathing regularly as she slept, and silence emanated from the Queen's chamber, yet Darya lay tensely, her eyes wide open. *What if the King is angered by Queen Esther's request?* she asked herself. *Master Haman will be right there. He knows how to manipulate the King. What if he turns the King against his wife?*

A picture floated into Darya's mind, of David telling her that Master Mordechai refused to bow before Master Haman, that Mordechai believed Haman had his own interests in mind rather than the King's. *But Master Haman will twist that around*, Darya thought in agitation. He would convince the King that Mordechai's not bowing to the King's Chief Minister meant that he and his people were not loyal. That was why they should be killed, and, of course, that was why their property should belong to the King and his supporters. Perhaps Haman would convince the King to arrest Mordechai right then, and David along with him!

Darya sat up quickly on her mat, her head spinning. She could no longer lie there tortured by her fears. She had to move. She needed fresh air. Quietly, she made her way out of the Queen's apartments and into her private garden. She breathed deeply of the moist earth and fragrant blossoms of springtime, and gazed up at the star-studded sky. But even that could not calm her tonight. She needed more space, more freedom to move. She let herself out of a small gate that put her outside of the cloistered walls of the women's quarters. Happily, the sentry on duty did not question her sudden appearance, most likely assuming she was on some errand for the Queen.

Darya followed a long, torchlit path that snaked along the walls of the palace. She was not paying much attention to where she was headed, just enjoying the quiet and the solitude, and trying to keep her mind as blank as possible. But suddenly she found herself entering the *paradaisia*, on the opposite side of the palace from where she had begun, and realized she was not far from the King's Gate and Master Mordechai's office. All of her worries and concerns crashed into her consciousness again, causing her to collapse onto a bench and put her head in her hands.

Twenty-Five

"Who are you? What are you doing here at this hour of the night?"

Darya's head jerked up. A young palace guard was standing over her, his hand on his sword grip. "I was just…." she stammered. "I only wanted to…." But she had no way of explaining why she was there.

The guard bent down to peer at her face in the torchlight. "I know you," he said more gently. "You serve the Queen. You are Parvaneh's friend. What are you doing here?"

It was Majeed, Darya realized, the new guard who always looked out for Parvaneh. "I am sorry," Darya apologized, standing up. "I know I should not be here. I will leave right now."

"Let me walk with you part of the way," Majeed said as Darya turned back toward the path. "It is well after midnight—not an hour that a young girl should be wandering the palace grounds alone."

She knew he was right. What had she been thinking? She pictured Behrooz and his companions, always cropping up unexpectedly along the palace paths. What if she had met them earlier tonight? She shuddered.

"Have you and Parvaneh worked together long?" Majeed asked companionably, falling into step beside her.

"We grew up together," Darya responded. "Not in the palace. We worked for an army captain who was killed in the Greek war."

"Ahh," Majeed said. "Then you know each other well." He cleared his throat and Darya could tell he was deciding whether to say something else. "Do you think," he began, before clearing his throat again. Finally, he said quickly, "Do you think I might have a chance with Parvaneh?"

"A chance with her?" Darya asked in a puzzled tone, although she understood exactly what he wanted to know. She turned her head aside and smiled secretly into the darkness.

"A chance," he repeated. "You know … to…." He broke off in confusion and Darya took pity on him.

"Yes," she said gently. "I think you have a good chance."

She turned back to him and saw that he was gazing up at the stars and smiling, and suddenly she grew very sad. Here were two young people wondering innocently if they had a chance at a life of happiness together, while this afternoon, the Judeans in the square were wondering if they had a chance at any life at all in the Empire. What chance had Monir had to grow up happily in her parents' home? What chance had the captain and all those other soldiers had to live through the Greek war? And what chance had she herself ever had to know who she really was, and to choose the kind of life she might want to lead? She wondered again about prayer, and hoped fervently that the gods were listening when people called out to them.

"I must caution you again," Majeed said, breaking into her thoughts. "What you did tonight was foolish. Even with palace guards on duty, it was truly not wise for you to wander the grounds alone in the dark—especially tonight, after the Judeans gathered in the square, and now all these rumors flying around."

"What rumors?" Darya asked tensely, as they continued along the path.

"You have not heard about the gallows?" he asked.

"Gallows?" she echoed, her fears spiraling skyward. "We heard nothing in the women's quarters. The Queen had a banquet. We were there all evening, with the King and the Chief Minister."

"The rumors are about the Minister and Master Mordechai," Majeed told her. "But perhaps I should not repeat them to you, what with you and Parvaneh always carrying messages between Master Mordechai and the Queen. Forgive me. I should not have spoken."

Darya halted abruptly and faced him. "Is Master Mordechai in some sort of danger? You must tell me, Majeed. The Queen would want to know."

"They are only rumors," Majeed said. "Nothing I saw for myself."

"Majeed, please!" Darya implored him.

She could see him debating with himself, until reluctantly he said, "When the Chief Minister left the banquet this evening, he left the palace through the King's Gate, as always. And as always, Master Mordechai refused to bow to him."

"That is no rumor," Darya countered. "It is nothing new."

"But this time, people are saying that the Minister could not control his rage. Perhaps it is because he had just been honored by the King and Queen, and here was Master Mordechai dishonoring him."

"What did he do?" Darya asked, not sure she wanted to know.

"They are saying that he marched home and met with his friends and his family—you know he has ten sons— and they convinced him it was time to put an end to the dishonor. They told him he was favored by the King and now by the Queen as well, and that Master Mordechai was dishonoring them as well as the Minister."

Majeed grew silent and began walking down the path again, but Darya refused to budge. "Finish, Majeed!" she demanded. "What else are people saying?"

He turned and looked at her unhappily. "That the Minister decided to build a very tall gallows right then and right there, near his house. His servants put it up for him earlier tonight. He plans to request that the King condemn Master Mordechai to death in the morning."

Darya felt nausea well up in her being. A gallows. A death sentence. "Majeed! The Queen must be told! I must run to the women's quarters!"

The two of them began racing down the path. They rounded the corner of the palace, heading toward the area that housed the King's apartments, and almost collided with a tall figure that suddenly loomed up before them.

"Who goes there?" demanded Majeed, panting loudly, his hand on his sword.

"I am Charbonah," came the response, "servant of the King." Darya remembered seeing him at the Queen's banquet.

"What is your business out here at this hour of the night?" asked Majeed.

"I am on an errand for the King," Charbonah responded, "and having little success." He peered at Majeed and then at Darya, who only wanted to continue running to the women's quarters. But a slow smile crept across Charbonah's face and he said, "Perhaps one of you can help me."

"One of *us*?" Majeed questioned. "We have important business. What is your errand?"

"The King is having trouble sleeping," Charbonah explained, keeping his eyes on Darya, as though to make sure she did not run off. "Instead of being relaxed by tonight's banquet with the Queen, all the food and drink is keeping him awake and agitated."

"And what is your errand?" Majeed repeated impatiently. "What are you searching for out here?"

"A scribe, sir," Charbonah replied. "The King wants someone who can read to him and lull him to sleep. I have been scouring the palace from end to end, but it seems all the scribes have disappeared tonight." He smiled at Darya and exclaimed, "Except for this one! You are the scribe of the women's quarters, am I not correct?"

"Yes, but…." Darya stammered as Charbonah firmly gripped her arm. "I am on my way to the Queen. I must go to her!"

Charbonah only gripped her arm more tightly. "I have no idea why you are running through the palace grounds at this hour, and I care not," he told her. "But you must come with me right now to read to the King."

Darya turned desperately to Majeed. "You must tell the Queen!" she admonished.

"I will try," he promised her. "But at this hour, and without you with me, I have little chance of delivering a message to the women's quarters."

Twenty-Six

King Xerxes was pacing his room like a Persian panther when Darya stepped into his chambers with Charbonah. A handful of tired servants and palace guards stood in an anteroom with concerned expressions on their faces. Darya bowed low at the entrance.

"What have you brought me?" the King demanded of his servant. "I ask for a scribe and you bring me a maiden!"

"Sire…." Charbonah began in a calming voice, but the King bellowed, "If I wanted a maiden, I would have sent you to the women's quarters! Get her out of my sight!"

Trembling and still bowing, Darya began backing out of the room, but Charbonah stopped her by gripping her arm again. "Sire," he repeated, in the same calming tone he had used before. "I brought what the King requested—a scribe—most likely one whose voice Your Majesty will find more soothing than the voices of most of the men found in the royal scriptorium."

Amazingly, the King stopped his pacing and his shouting. Charbonah had known just how to speak to him, Darya realized. She was even more amazed to hear the King give a short laugh. "You might be right, my man, as always," he said. "Let me have a look at her." Turning to Darya, he said, "Rise, girl."

As Darya straightened, the King exclaimed, "You are one of the Queen's handmaidens! You were at the feast tonight."

"Yes, Your Majesty," Darya whispered, still shaken by his display of temper. *How does Queen Esther live with him, never knowing what to expect from one minute to the next?* she wondered.

"How is it that you can read and write?" the King demanded. "You are only a servant, and a female one, at that."

Darya kept her eyes lowered respectfully and said, "I was taught alongside my young mistress, sire, so that I could help her with her lessons."

The King laughed. "This grows more interesting by the moment, Charbonah," he remarked, before turning back to Darya. "And why, pray tell, was your young mistress learning to read and write, when not even the King himself has been taught?"

"My master was a captain in Your Majesty's army, sire," Darya explained. "He traveled the world and believed that reading and writing are important skills. He wanted his daughter to have them, in case she ever needed to run a household alone or a business to support herself."

"An interesting man, this captain of mine," the King commented. "He was certainly listening closely when we praised our courageous ally Artimesia in Greece. We said that our women were becoming like men and our men were becoming like women—and it seems your captain was raising a daughter as though she were a son! I would like to meet him. Where is he now?"

Darya's answer stuck in her throat. How could she say that the captain was killed in Greece? That would conjure up the failed war, and all the dead soldiers, and the high taxes that were still being levied to pay for the debacle. But the King had asked her a direct question. "The captain did not return from Greece, sire," Darya said softly.

She waited for the King's anger to erupt, but he remained silent. He turned away from her and stepped to a window, pushing aside its silk draperies and staring out at the black night. Finally, he turned back and walked to a couch, where he reclined on gem-colored cushions. "Read to me, girl," he said gruffly. "That is why you are here."

Darya looked around in confusion, wondering what she was supposed to read. She turned to Charbonah inquiringly, and he led her to a low stool a few feet away from the King's couch. Then he brought her a huge basket filled with scrolls. "These are from the palace library. They are records of happenings in the Empire." He smiled very slightly and whispered, "Very good for helping the King fall asleep."

Darya fingered the scrolls and noticed that each one had a clay tag dangling from one end. She looked toward the King. "Sire, shall I read the tags to Your Majesty so that the King might choose a scroll?"

The King wagged his hand at her irritably. "Choose anything," he grumbled. "Just read, already."

Darya quickly rummaged through the scrolls. She avoided anything that had to do with the Greek war or taxes, and was relieved when she found one recording the birth of Crown Prince Artaxerxes. That sounded like a safe, even pleasant, subject. Unrolling the scroll, she began to read about the day and time of the baby's birth, his weight and length, along with the names of all the nobles who were in attendance in the anterooms at the time of the delivery. This was followed by a listing of the baby's parents, grandparents, and ancestors, extending further back than even the founding of the Empire. Darya's choice of reading matter was rewarded by a small smile on the King's face, as well as a more relaxed attitude as he lay on the couch.

When she finished the scroll, Darya quickly searched for another to replace it, hoping to prevent the King from becoming irritated again. She chose one that detailed how the King's father, Darius, had come to the throne. He had deposed a usurper named Smerdis, who had grabbed power when Cambyses, the son of Cyrus "the Great," had died mysteriously. As she read, she remembered sitting at the captain's kitchen table, listening to Nasim tell this same story to her, and to Jaleh and Parvaneh. It was right after Monir had left for Persepolis with her relatives, soon after they had learned of the captain's death. Darya marveled at how much had happened since then. It seemed like another lifetime.

She glanced over at the King and saw that his eyes were closed, and so she replaced the scroll and sat quietly, wondering whether Charbonah would give her permission to leave and go to the Queen. She was suddenly very tired and longed to deliver her message and return to her mat in the women's quarters. Her shoulders sagged and her eyelids drooped as she sat on the stool, but she jumped guiltily at the sound of the King's voice. "Read!" he ordered, even though his eyes were still closed. "Why did you stop?"

Quickly, she searched through the basket again, until one of the tags caught her eye and sent a chill up her spine. It said "Bigthan and Teresh," the names of the courtiers who had plotted against the King and were hanged soon after the Lady Esther had become Queen—the courtiers whose plot had been exposed by Master Mordechai. Darya did not think this was the best topic to choose to relax the King, but she realized it might be just what the King needed to hear before the Chief Minister requested Mordechai's execution. And it might be what the King had to hear before his second banquet with the Queen, when she planned to ask him to save Master Mordechai and the Judeans.

Jaleh's long-ago words, that the gods put everyone where they were for a reason, floated back to Darya. Was this why she hadn't been able to sleep on her mat in the Queen's quarters? Was this why she had collided with Charbonah on the path? With shaking hands, Darya unrolled the scroll and began to read.

When she finished, she was certain Queen Esther had a hand in how the story had been told. In fact, Darya would not have been surprised to learn that the Queen had actually dictated the account to the scribes. The part that the Queen had played in the incident was described in very few words, while Master Mordechai's actions were highlighted and praised abundantly: how he had overheard the courtiers plotting near the King's Gate; how he had immediately informed the Queen; how his quick response had surely saved the King's life. Darya prayed that her choice of the scroll would help the people she cared about, but she was bitterly disappointed when she looked over at the King. He had most likely slept through the entire reading.

Dejectedly, she replaced the scroll in the basket and glanced at Charbonah, who was sitting half asleep on the floor, leaning against the foot of the King's couch. She was trapped in the King's chambers and wondered if she too might slide to the floor, lean her head on the stool, and close her eyes. But once again, the King's voice surprised her and made her jump. "Is that the end of the scroll?" he asked.

"Yes, sire," Darya responded, straightening up on the stool. She expected him to demand that she continue reading, but instead he asked, "Is there not some notation about how Master Mordechai was rewarded for saving the life of the King?"

Darya unrolled the scroll again to examine it. "No, sire," she said. "There is nothing about a reward."

"Well, that must be remedied!" the King exclaimed, to Darya's delight. He was fully awake once more and commented, "I must speak with my advisors and hear some suggestions." He glanced toward the window, where the first glimmer of dawn traced the edges of the silk curtains with light. "Charbonah!" he barked, and the exhausted servant jumped to his feet.

"Yes, sire. My apologies, sire."

"Stop your apologizing and go to the anterooms. See if any of my ministers are early risers. If anyone is about, bring him in here at once."

Who would be about at this hour? Darya wondered. It was barely dawn. No one would be stirring in the Queen's chambers, either. Had Majeed been able to deliver the message? She doubted it. She also doubted that Charbonah would find anyone in the anterooms, and so she gasped and nearly lost her balance on the stool when he returned with two men close behind him: Chief Minister Haman, and Master Behrooz attending him!

"Perfect! My Chief Minister!" the King exclaimed, rising from his couch.

Charbonah moved into the shadows against the wall near the window and gestured to Darya to join him there. They watched as Haman and Behrooz bowed low to the King.

Haman's face was beaming at the welcome he had received. He had hardly noticed Darya in the room, but Behrooz's expression was surprised and confused, and his eyes kept wandering to the shadows where Darya stood. He was obviously wondering why she was there, and, knowing him, Darya suspected he was also trying to gauge whether her presence in the King's chambers could be used to his advantage in some way. She was not surprised when he positioned himself near her and Charbonah, but also close enough to the King and Haman to be able to follow their conversation.

He is very good at what he does, Darya thought with grudging admiration. *He gathers bits and pieces of information like pebbles on a beach. He misses nothing. I can understand why Master Haman and Master Arman value his services and want him nearby.*

"Haman, we have had a restless night," the King was saying.

"That is unfortunate, sire," Haman responded in a soothing voice. "Perhaps I can be of service to help the King relax."

"Perhaps you can," the King responded. He began his animal-like pacing again and said, "We have been trying to solve a problem, to right a wrong."

"Your Majesty always aims to do what is just," Haman said.

"What is just," the King repeated. "You always seem to know precisely the word that is called for!" He stopped his pacing abruptly and smiled at Haman. "If one of our subjects has not received the honor he justly deserves, what can be done about that? What should be done for a man whom the King desires to honor?"

"Excellent," Darya heard Behrooz mutter to himself. He turned to her with his sinister smile and murmured under his breath, "The King wants Haman to be honored. It is the end for your great Master Mordechai!"

The familiar sensation of icy fingers encircling her neck made Darya struggle for breath. She knew that the King had intended to honor Master Mordechai, but was it possible that Haman would turn the tables? Was his influence over the King so powerful that he could manipulate him to bestow upon Haman the honor that the King had wanted to shower on Mordechai? And what of those gallows? She knew what Haman wanted to request of the King. She was sure he had been awake the entire night planning this early morning meeting. Would he be able to turn the King against the man who had saved his life?

"Speak, man!" the King demanded of his Minister. "What is the best way for us to honor a deserving subject?"

"Sire," Haman began with a pleased smile, obviously believing like Behrooz that the King wished to honor him. "Everyone knows that Your Majesty is the most honored being in the Empire, and therefore permitting one of Your Majesty's subjects to look and act like the King— temporarily, of course—would be the greatest honor Your Majesty could bestow."

"Explain yourself, sir," the King demanded. "How would this subject look and act like the King?"

"Ahh," Haman replied, glancing at Behrooz, his smile even broader. "Let this man wear clothing that the King has worn. And let this man ride a horse that the King has ridden. And let this man wear the crown that rests on the King's head!"

Darya was appalled by Haman's suggestions, and, looking at the King's expression, she could see that he was taken aback as well. This was far more than bestowing honor upon a subject; this was almost transferring power!

But Haman was not finished. He was still smiling broadly and seemed totally entranced by the vision he was creating. "Then assign a chief noble of the realm, perhaps one of those like Master Mordechai who sit in the King's Gate, to lead this crowned subject upon the King's horse. Let the noble parade the horse and rider through the square, proclaiming, 'This is what is done for a man whom the King wishes to honor!'"

The room grew still. Haman stood flushed and triumphant before the King, seeming oblivious to the fact that the King was not smiling with him. The King's jaw was taut and his eyes blazed, and Darya wondered if he would fly into one of his rages. But then she saw him gradually relax, as he had when she read to him, and a slow smile finally spread across his face.

"Excellent plan! Excellent!" the King intoned. "You must follow your plan to the letter."

Haman nodded almost giddily, until the King added, "Charbonah will supply everything you need. Bring the clothing, the horse, and the crown to Master Mordechai in the King's Gate, and you are to lead him around the square, exactly as you described. Do it today!"

Haman stared at the King in disbelief, as did Behrooz. Haman's mouth opened and closed several times, but he could form no words. The King, meanwhile, was looking very pleased with himself. At last Haman motioned to Behrooz to join him before the King. They both seemed to shrink and crumple as they bowed low and took their leave.

Twenty-Seven

"Darya, it is time to wake up. We must prepare for the second banquet," Parvaneh said softly. She shook Darya's shoulder as the girl napped on her mat in the Queen's anteroom. When Esther had heard Darya's message and learned that the girl had been awake the entire night, she had insisted that Darya rest for a few hours before attending her at the feast.

"Leave me be," Darya begged, pushing Parvaneh's hand away. "I was having such wonderful dreams about Master Mordechai on the King's horse in the square this afternoon."

"It was wonderful, was it not?" Parvaneh agreed, crouching on the floor beside Darya. "One day Master Mordechai is in sackcloth and ashes, and the next he is dressed like the King. I could almost feel sorry for Master Haman. He was so humiliated leading that horse around the square."

"I, too, could *almost* feel sorry for him," Darya agreed, rising and rolling up her mat, "until I thought about the scroll Master Mordechai showed me in the square, and about the gallows. If the King had not decided to honor Master Mordechai, then Master Haman would have been requesting his death. Your friend Majeed told me the gallows were just a rumor, but there were people in the square who had actually seen them."

Parvaneh's face turned pink. "Majeed is not my friend," she murmured. "He just—"

"He just looks out for you," Darya laughed, finishing Parvaneh's sentence. "I know, I know. But he would like very much to be your friend."

"How do you know that?" Parvaneh asked. "What did he say to you?"

Darya put her hands on Parvaneh's shoulders and smiled. "He asked if he had 'a chance' with you, and I told him he did."

"You said that?" Parvaneh whispered, and Darya nodded. "Then you must also tell him to speak to my mother," Parvaneh said, trying to suppress a smile. "That is the proper way."

"We will be sure to do this the proper way," Darya promised. "But now we must go to the Queen and help her prepare for her feast."

∞

The scene in the Queen's dining chamber was almost a repeat of the night before, with the Queen, the King, and the Chief Minister reclining on their ornate couches, superb food and drink arranged on small gilt tables before them. But the atmosphere of the banquet had changed. The three participants seemed wary of each other and on guard.

From her place in the shadows near Parvaneh and Hasach, Darya could see that the Chief Minister ate almost nothing. He kept glancing at the King almost fearfully, as though trying to gauge what his standing was now, after the humiliation the King had put him through that afternoon.

Queen Esther ate very little, as well. She was tense, Darya knew, since this evening was when she was going to plead for Master Mordechai and the Judeans. The fact that Mordechai had just been honored was certainly helpful, but there was still the scroll, which detailed the death sentence for the Judeans and the confiscation of their property.

The King, on the other hand, ate and drank well, although not as heartily as he had the previous evening. He, too, seemed tense and preoccupied. When he looked at his Chief Minister, it seemed to Darya that she could see a shadow of the way the King had scrutinized the Minister early that morning, when Haman had first made the suggestion of dressing a subject as the King. Darya thought she could see distrust and dislike in the King's expression, not at all the way the King had always regarded his Minister in the past. He kept examining Haman's face, as though searching for a window into the Minister's true plans and desires.

At last the King turned to Esther and his expression changed to one of affection. He said kindly, "Well, our lovely Queen, you have wined and dined us well, but you have yet to make a request of us. What is it that you wish? As we have already said, we are prepared to bestow upon you up to half the kingdom, if that is what you desire."

Esther gazed at her husband with a mixture of sadness and dread. "The Queen is so afraid," Darya whispered to Parvaneh, who nodded. They were both aware that the Queen knew better than almost anyone how abruptly the King's mood could change, and how violent he could become. Finally, Esther slid off her couch and, as Haman watched uneasily, she half-crouched and half-bowed before the King.

"Sire," she murmured. "The King has always been more than generous, and I have no desire for land or riches. My request...."

It seemed to Darya that Esther's voice had faded along with her courage. But the King placed his jeweled hand beneath her chin and gently raised her face toward him. "Speak, Esther," he murmured encouragingly. "What is it that you wish?"

She looked into his eyes, took a deep breath, and said in a shaky voice, "My wish is for the King to grant me my life, and my request is for the King to grant the lives of my people." The expressions on both the King's face and Haman's were bewildered, and she continued, "I and my people have been sold! We are to be destroyed and murdered and utterly lost!"

Everyone in the chamber stared at the Queen in confusion, from Darya, Parvaneh and Hasach in the shadows on one side of the room, to Charbonah and the other royal servants in the shadows on the other side of the room, to the soldiers of the palace guard stationed near the entrance, to the two powerful men on the couches. Both the King and the Minister sat up straight and leaned toward the crouching Queen. The King demanded, "What is this all about? Who is it who dares to threaten you and your people?"

Very slowly, Esther twisted away from the King and faced the Chief Minister. Her voice no longer shook as she stated very clearly, "My enemy and the enemy of my people is this evil man, Haman!"

For a few moments the room was deathly silent as the onlookers digested the Queen's words and what they meant. Then, suddenly, it was as though the chamber shuddered in an earthquake as everyone spoke and moved at once, turning to their neighbors, repeating what the Queen had said, identifying her as a Judean, reviewing what had been written in Haman's scroll, and wondering how the King would react.

The servants and soldiers watched as both the King and Haman jumped up, knocking over the food-laden tables before them. They stared at each other, an expression of uncontrollable rage on the King's face, and one of pure terror on the Minister's. Everyone braced themselves for the King's furious tirade that was sure to erupt, but instead, the King turned toward Esther and examined her intently, staring into her eyes as though trying to penetrate her soul.

He no longer knows who she is, Darya realized with sudden comprehension. *If she is Judean, is she still the same woman he married—the same woman who enchanted him years ago, and became Queen of Susa, and bore his heir?*

Esther remained perfectly still, returning his gaze, not

explaining, not pleading, simply looking at him steadily and allowing him whatever time he needed. The whole room was frozen; no one dared move, not even Haman. They were waiting for the King to act. With an effort, he finally shifted his eyes away from Esther; then he brushed roughly past his Minister and his palace guard, and stalked from the room into the Queen's garden.

Darya watched the Queen drag herself slowly back onto her couch. Esther moved like an old woman, as though all of her energy had been sapped by the revelations she had just made, and by the way the King had scrutinized her. She lay back on her cushions in exhaustion and closed her eyes, just as Haman dropped to his knees beside her and grabbed the sleeve of her gown.

"Your Majesty, please, you must help me…." he pleaded in a trembling voice. "This is all a mistake."

Esther's eyes flew open to see the Minister's face close to hers. Desperately, she shifted to the far side of her couch and tried to pry his fingers from her sleeve, but he would not let go. He sprawled across the couch, begging for her help. Then suddenly he grew rigid with fear as the King's voice bellowed from the doorway, "You dare to attack the Queen right before us in our own palace?!"

Haman spun around on his knees to face the King. "Never, sire! By the gods! Please! I would never—"

But the palace guard had descended upon him and dragged him to his feet. "We await Your Majesty's orders," the captain of the guard said to the King.

Darya held her breath, waiting for the King to respond. She saw him looking toward the couch, where Esther had struggled to a sitting position. Esther gazed at her husband with a questioning expression on her face, but also one of resignation. Would the King still accept her as his Queen? Would he protect her people? Or would he choose to forgive his Minister and reinstate his power?

Almost imperceptibly, the King nodded at Esther, and Darya could see the tension leave her body. Then the King turned to the guards holding Haman. "Get him out of our sight," he growled, his rage returning, "while we decide what to do with this Minister, who desired our horse and our clothing and our very crown, and now goes after our Queen!"

Darya let out her breath in relief as the guards began dragging Haman toward the doorway. Then she saw Charbonah step from the shadows across the room from her. "Sire," he said in the calming voice that Darya was well aware he knew how to use to quiet the King's anger.

"Speak!" the King ordered.

"Sire," Charbonah repeated. "There is a tall gallows. The Chief Minister had it built for Master Mordechai—he who saved the King. It stands near the Chief Minister's house."

Very slowly the King regained his composure. "Well said, Charbonah," he rasped. "Well said." He nodded meaningfully again, but this time to the captain of the guard, who hauled Haman from the room.

Twenty-Eight

Susa was the same capital city in the Empire, but not the same. It was ruled by the same King and Queen, but not the same. "It is as though the stars shifted to different positions in the sky," Parvaneh remarked to Darya, gazing at the heavens as they took a break in the Queen's garden several evenings later. "Same stars, same sky, but so much has changed!"

"I know," Darya agreed. "We serve the same Queen as before, but it is different now. It feels like she is inside a closed circle with Master Mordechai and David and all the Judeans in the Empire, and we are on the outside."

"At least now we know why each of the Queen's handmaidens performed different jobs on different days," Parvaneh laughed. "That mystery is solved."

Darya smiled. "It was very clever of our Queen, do you not agree?"

Parvaneh nodded. "The way I understand it, it was her way of keeping track of the days of the week and observing the Judean Sabbath properly. She figured out how to light her Sabbath candles and not violate the rules of her religion, with no one being the wiser. She simply lit the lamps in her room herself on the sixth day, as though they were Sabbath candles, and left them for us to light on the seventh when the Sabbath rules prevented her from lighting any candles at all."

"I believe that is so," Darya agreed.

The girls wandered down a winding garden path, fragrant with a border of roses. Darya continued to sift through the events of the past few days in her mind: how the Chief Minister was hanged for treason; how people learned that Master Mordechai was related to the Queen, and that he had raised her when she was orphaned as a child; how Master Mordechai was put in charge of the vast properties that had been owned by Haman; and how he was now a chief advisor to both the King and Queen. But something still troubled Darya, something had not yet been resolved. "What of the scroll?" she asked Parvaneh.

"What scroll?" Parvaneh replied blankly.

"The scroll that Master Mordechai showed me that day in the square—the scroll that ordered death for the Judeans. Have you heard anything more about it? Are the Judeans, and the Queen, completely safe now?"

The girls received their answer when they returned to the Queen's apartments and were immediately summoned to Esther's audience hall, where she was in serious conversation with Master Mordechai. Darya's heart skipped a beat when she saw that David was also in attendance.

"Take pen and ink and papyrus," the Queen ordered her handmaidens, indicating a stack of writing implements on a side table. "We are drafting a letter that must be sent immediately to all the satrapies—the provinces—of the Empire. Write as clearly as you can so that the King's scribes can make accurate copies and translations."

Darya and Parvaneh took seats at the table across from David, who sat ready to write. The girls arranged their sheets of papyrus, reed pens, and clay jars of ink, and waited for further instructions from the Queen and Master Mordechai.

"I still fail to understand why the King insists he cannot help us any further," Esther said bitterly to Mordechai, a worried frown creasing her brow. "He was willing to hand me half the kingdom, yet he cannot cancel the edict that is like an avalanche waiting to crush every Judean living in the Empire."

"Hush," Mordechai cautioned her, glancing around the room. "Criticizing the King is never wise. He is only following the law of the land, that an edict sealed by the King cannot be revoked. Instead, he is allowing us to send out a new edict—the one that we will dictate right now—that announces that all Judeans are permitted to take up arms against anyone who attacks them. That should cause anyone contemplating an attack to think twice before acting."

"But what if Judeans are attacked anyway?" Esther asked tensely, rubbing her face with her hands. "We are hearing reports that Haman's supporters are in every city of the Empire. Those that used to follow him around, like that Behrooz, have scattered to all the satrapies. We hear that Haman's ten sons are out to avenge their father. We hear that his followers still believe what he told them: that we Judeans are not trustworthy, that we are harmful to the Empire, that we have jobs that are rightfully theirs, and that we own property for the taking. They are eager to attack and to kill and to plunder. They only wait for the day that Haman designated for this massacre!"

The room grew very still when Esther stopped speaking. Darya's heart pounded in fear as she stole a glance at David and thought about the danger surrounding these people who meant so much to her. Finally, Mordechai said, "Perhaps that is precisely why the King is allowing Judeans to defend themselves on that day. He *wants* a Judean defense because he allowed Haman's followers to arm themselves, and now he realizes his mistake: that they are eager to attack not just the Judeans, but anyone who opposes them—perhaps even the King himself."

Mordechai thought for a moment, then continued, "Possibly the King needs people to rise up and fight for him against Haman's supporters. They believe, as he did, that the chosen day has special meaning—that it was designated by their gods through lots that he cast, and so it will bring them special favor. Remember, Haman is the man who wanted to wear the King's crown. The King did not trust him then, and he does not trust his followers now."

∞

During the months that followed, Darya was happier than she could ever remember being. She knew it was strange that she should be so happy when the people she cared most about were in danger, but it was the danger that had led to this happiness!

The Queen's audience hall had become the center for planning how to protect the Judeans of the Empire. This meant that the apartments were always busy with messengers coming and going, with Judean leaders from all the far-flung satrapies of the Empire arriving to meet with the Queen, with Master Mordechai always in attendance, and, of course, with David always there assisting him.

Darya and Parvaneh were constantly needed to write messages, run errands, and attend the Queen. They were not part of the inner circle of Judeans, but they were firmly entrenched in the outer circle made up of the myriads of Persians who wanted to be part of the Judean camp. Now that it was known that the Queen was Judean, and that the King favored her and granted the right of arms to her people, it had become fashionable—and politically valuable—to become a member of that outer circle.

But for Darya it was much more than being part of the Judean camp. "I feel like I am part of a family," she whispered to Parvaneh late one night when they had collapsed in exhaustion on their mats in the corner of the Queen's anteroom. "I do not remember my family, but now I feel like I am part of one that includes you and David and the Queen and Master Mordechai... and even little Artaxerxes." She sighed. "I wish ... If only...."

"If only what?" Parvaneh prompted.

Darya sighed again and said almost inaudibly, "If only this could go on forever, and not be connected to this danger hanging over the Judeans."

Parvaneh reached over and touched her shoulder. "You must talk to the Queen," she urged. "You must tell her your feelings for David—as if anyone who notices how your face lights up when you see him would not know!" Parvaneh giggled softly.

"I cannot talk to the Queen," Darya protested. "Not now. Not until this danger is passed. Just like you have told your mother not to ask Master Arman to speak to the Queen about Majeed until all of this is over."

"I suppose you are right," Parvaneh conceded. "But at least my mother knows about Majeed. It is a small step, but at least it is something. You must do something too."

"I am trying!" Darya protested. "You know I am trying. Whenever there is time, I borrow scrolls from the palace library that have to do with the Judeans. I am learning so much about their religion, and about their history." She began reciting, as though she were back helping Monir with her lessons. "Long ago, they were slaves of the Egyptians, just like I am a slave here. They escaped Egypt and made their way to Canaan, a land promised to them by their God. But their land was conquered and their great Temple destroyed by the Babylonians, and they were marched into exile in Babylon. Then they were freed from captivity by the Persians and were told they could return to their land and rebuild their Temple. But the building was stopped when other residents of Judea complained about it, and now they are waiting to be allowed to build again."

Frustrated, Darya sat up and stared through the darkness at her friend. "I am trying, but we have so little free time, as you know. And there is so much I do not know about them, and so much I do not understand."

"You could ask David to explain things to you," Parvaneh suggested soothingly. "He should at least know what you are doing, and that you are interested."

"I have asked him about some things," Darya replied more calmly, lying down again. "He always smiles and says he is pleased at my interest. But usually we are both so busy assisting the Queen and Master Mordechai."

"At least he knows," Parvaneh murmured tiredly. "It is a start. And remember, he always smiles."

Twenty-Nine

Just a few days later, Darya returned to the apartments after a morning spent with Hasach doing various errands for the Queen. She was met by Parvaneh, who motioned her into the anteroom, her face beaming. Darya's heart fluttered, thinking this had something to do with their conversation about David, but Parvaneh hurried to the corner of the anteroom where they had left their rolled sleeping mats. She bent down to pick up a scroll that was lying there and waved it gaily at Darya.

"From Monir!" she exclaimed happily. "It arrived this morning while you were out. A group of Judeans brought it from Persepolis, and I was waiting for you to come back so we could enjoy it together."

The girls made themselves comfortable on the rolled mats against the wall as Parvaneh broke the seal on the scroll. She flattened it on her lap and began to read, with Darya looking over her shoulder.

"*My Dear Friends,*" Parvaneh read. "*As soon as I heard that a group of Judeans was traveling to Susa to meet with Queen Esther, I rushed to write this letter for them to deliver to you.*"

Darya smiled at how smoothly and confidently Parvaneh could read now, after all the written work she had been doing for the Queen.

Parvaneh continued, "*One of the men in the group is the merchant I wrote to you about, the father of my new friend, Leah—you know, the girl that I think resembles Darya—and I knew he would get this to you safely.*"

"Did you meet him?" Darya asked Parvaneh. "Leah's father? Did he hand you the scroll?"

Parvaneh nodded. "After meeting with the Queen and Master Mordechai, he surprised everyone by making a special request to be introduced to two of the Queen's handmaidens—to us—but of course, I was the only one here. He did not just hand me the scroll. He wanted to know what I did and where I was from and especially how I had learned to read and write. He said that he thinks so highly of his daughter's friend Monir that he wanted to meet Monir's other friends, as well."

"I am sorry I missed him," Darya murmured. "He sounds like a fine man, calling us her friends, when he must know we are not really her equal."

"You can ask David about him," Parvaneh responded. "Leah's father spent quite some time talking to David also. They actually took a walk together in the Queen's garden."

Darya raised her eyebrows in surprise. "I will ask David about it," she said. "But let us read more of the letter."

Parvaneh leaned over the scroll again and continued reading what Monir had written:

Life in Persepolis is full of rumors and fears. I am sure it is the same everywhere else in the Empire, especially in Susa.

Until all this talk of fighting and attacks is over, life will not be normal again. Since I am friends with Leah, I see more of the Judeans than my cousins, and I am frightened for them. The King has allowed them to take up arms to defend themselves and they are doing that very seriously. Leah's home is one of many places where money is being raised for weapons. They are being bought and collected there, and sometimes I see young men practicing swordplay in her garden! It is awful to watch, and awful to think that Master Haman's followers are probably doing exactly the same thing. And in a few months, all of them might be having real swordplay against each other.

Parvaneh stopped reading and sat back in silence. Next to her, Darya said nothing, imagining what Monir was seeing. Finally, Darya whispered, "We do not see the swords here. We see the meetings and the planning, but not the swordplay. Monir has made it all so much more scary."

Parvaneh nodded. "But they are preparing, which is what they must do. They are preparing all over the Empire."

The girls sat lost in their thoughts until finally Darya took the scroll from Parvaneh's lap to finish reading it. Monir had written:

Our lives just seem to be waiting. My aunt and uncle say they will wait to consider suitors for me until after these troubles are over, and Leah's parents have said the same thing to her. But at least this waiting gives me time to write to you and to remember the happiness we once had together.

> *I miss you and hope you are both well, along with Madame*
> *Jaleh and Nasim.*
> *Monir*

Darya rerolled the papyrus thoughtfully. "Do you suppose we will ever see her again?" she asked Parvaneh. "All of us thinking about marriage. All of us waiting for other people to make the decisions that will change our lives. Troubles in the Empire." She turned to her friend. "What do you think will happen?"

"Only the gods know," Parvaneh sighed, sounding like her mother. Slowly, she rose to her feet. "But for now, I am certain the Queen has work for us to do, and that she is wondering where we are."

As soon as the girls returned to the Queen's audience hall, they were set to work writing more of Master Mordechai's documents for the King's scribes to copy and send out to all the satrapies. Darya concentrated on writing neat and clear symbols, but she was acutely aware of David sitting across the table from her. She did not dare even to glance at him, afraid of becoming distracted and leaving out an important word or phrase. Abruptly, though, Master Mordechai stopped dictating. A new group of Judeans had entered the audience hall and he went to greet them and speak with them.

Darya, Parvaneh, and David straightened on their stools and tiredly rubbed their necks and their eyes. They looked at each other and smiled. "Who would have thought just writing could be so tiring," David murmured.

The girls nodded. "It is because of what we are writing," Parvaneh responded softly. "And because we want to make sure we write it perfectly."

They all looked over to where Master Mordechai was in deep conversation with the party of Judeans. Their voices were low, their expressions serious, and it made Darya think of Monir's letter and her description of the weapons being collected and the swordplay in the garden. Hesitantly, she turned to David. "Parvaneh told me there were Judeans here from Persepolis this morning," she said.

He looked at her and nodded. "One of the men asked to meet you," he said.

"Yes," she replied. "Parvaneh told me. She said the man wanted to talk to you too."

David was silent a moment, then looked down at the papyrus on the table. He picked up his reed pen and rolled it between his fingers. "We spoke," he said finally. "We walked in the Queen's garden. He asked me where I was from, and about my family, and what I did for Master Mordechai. He seems like a fine man."

Darya thought he was about to say more, but he stopped. She gazed at him across the table, thinking he looked troubled, but he did not look up. And he did not smile.

∞

From that day on, David rarely smiled at Darya, and when he did, he looked uncomfortable and even unhappy. Darya wanted to ask him what was wrong, but did not know how to phrase the question. Every so often, she was sure he wanted to tell her something. He would look at her intently, even open his mouth to speak, but then he would turn away and busy himself with any task at hand.

And all the while, time marched forward, very much like an attacking army trampling over summer, autumn, and winter. Letters were written, money was transferred, weapons were distributed, strategies were planned. The days, weeks, and months passed, and the early spring target date arranged by Haman was upon them.

After all the urgent meetings and errands and letter-writing, the Queen's chambers grew strangely subdued and still. She asked for Artaxerxes to be brought to her and took the toddler into her garden to play with him on the fragrant spring grass. She picked him up and hugged him tightly, burrowing her face in his neck and shoulder, before sending him back to his rooms with his nursemaids. Then she turned to Mordechai, David, Darya, and Parvaneh, the only people she had not dismissed from her audience hall.

"We have done all we can," she said quietly, looking at each of them in turn. "All that is humanly possible." She lowered her head. "The only thing we can do now is pray."

Mordechai nodded silently and signaled to David to follow him from the room. Esther turned away and entered an inner chamber. And Darya and Parvaneh made their way into the Queen's garden, each of them following a separate path through the dusk.

Thirty

Messengers began arriving in the Queen's chambers early the next morning with reports of what was happening in Susa and, as the dreadful day wore on, with accounts of events in further reaches of the Empire. Haman's followers had wasted no time. The attacks had begun with the first light—and so had the resistance.

In the safety of the Queen's chambers, encircled by the palace and its walls and its guards, Darya, Parvaneh, and David recorded the events as they were reported: a Judean shop looted and burned to the ground; a Judean home ransacked; Judeans wounded as they defended a neighborhood. Darya and Parvaneh tensed every time a report came in from Persepolis, fearing that Monir and her relatives might have been caught up in the fighting, or that Monir's friends had been targeted, since their home was a center for Judean defense.

But the three young scribes also recorded that Haman's attacking men were blocked from entering a Judean area by armed Judeans and Persians; that a pitched street battle had left the ground littered with wounded and dying attackers; that groups of Haman's men were taken prisoner; that others were fleeing from the cities into the surrounding hillsides.

The messengers kept coming from the closer satrapies in a horribly steady stream, and the recorded lists grew longer and bloodier. Everyone in the Queen's chambers knew that the King's scribes were assembled in their own war room and were compiling their own lists, but Esther refused to rely on second-hand information. After all, the fate of her people was on the line. Mordechai shuttled between the King's chambers and the Queen's, making sure that both had accurate details.

Eventually, David was assigned to record only Judean casualties, while Darya and Parvaneh kept track of the fate of Haman's attacking army, as the day blundered into dusk and then darkness. When it was followed by a lackluster sun seeming to rise against its will to shed light on new scenes of destruction, David sat idle more and more, while Darya and Parvaneh filled scroll after scroll of papyrus. As darkness descended a second time, though, Darya and Parvaneh laid down their reed pens as well, and the three young people rested their heads on the table in exhaustion.

"It seems to be over," Esther murmured, "although I am sure we will be hearing from the further satrapies for days." She leaned over the table to scan some of the lists, especially running her finger down the notations David had made about attacks in Susa; then she turned slowly away and collapsed onto a couch. "The attackers have been routed." But there was no jubilation in her voice, only sadness and fatigue. "So much harm. So much hatred." She covered her eyes with a trembling hand. "How will we all move forward after this?"

The room was silent until Mordechai said quietly, "We will move forward as any kingdom does after a war." He sighed. "Because this was a war—a civil war—with one large group of citizens pitted against another. Thank Heaven it lasted only two days."

"But it is not really over, is it?" David asked tiredly, raising his head from the table. "What of all the prisoners who were taken? What of all the attackers hiding in the hills?"

"Many of those in hiding will be rounded up in the next few weeks," Mordechai agreed somberly. "And there will be trials, with exile for some, and prison or hangings for others."

"Hangings," Parvaneh echoed with a shudder, lifting her head. "More death. I wish it could just be over."

"Oh, there will be some clemency," Mordechai assured her. "The King will do his best to pardon as many as he can to promote peace and good feeling. And there will be some who find ways to bargain their way out of prison. But what would you do with the leaders? What would you do with Haman's sons, who will never stop trying to avenge their father? What would you do with Haman's close circle, like that man Behrooz, who attacked you at the King's Gate?"

Instead of answering, Parvaneh laid her head on the table again and covered it with her hands, as though trying to shut out the truth of Mordechai's words.

It was Darya's turn to raise her head. "Do we know if Monir is safe, and her friend's family?"

David answered in a weary voice, "A rider from Persepolis came late this afternoon with a message from Leah's father. It is on my list. All is well in their community."

"Thankfully," Darya murmured, and then she asked, "Do we know what happened to Master Behrooz? It would be comforting to know that he will never be harming any of us again."

"You are protected here," Queen Esther assured her. "If he is found, he will be imprisoned, and possibly worse. You need not fear him."

Darya nodded gratefully, but until Behrooz was located, she knew she would not feel entirely safe.

∞

The aftermath of the uprising was not pretty. Darya and Parvaneh could not leave the palace grounds without seeing bound and battered prisoners being marched through the streets, or crowds of people with picnic baskets and a holiday mood off to watch a hanging.

"Why would they want to see it?" Parvaneh asked with a shudder, as she and Darya hurried through the square on their way back to the palace from an errand. "And why would they bring their children along?"

Darya shrugged. "I have never understood it, but maybe they are celebrating the end of something evil ... or maybe they are just relieved that someone else is suffering and they are safe."

"I heard that hundreds came to watch when Master Haman's sons were hanged," Parvaneh said, while they waited their turn to be permitted to enter the palace grounds past all the extra guards now on duty. "Majeed was there, but not with a picnic basket. He told me he felt he should be there out of loyalty to the King and Queen, to show how much he was against what Master Haman stood for."

"Majeed?" Darya asked, peering closely at her friend. "You have been speaking to Majeed? Is there something you have not told me?"

Parvaneh's face turned pink as she ducked into the shadows of the King's Gate when they were finally allowed through. Darya hurried after her. "What have you not told me?" she demanded, panting.

Parvaneh stopped and faced her friend. She smiled shyly. "My mother has spoken to Master Arman. He has agreed to speak to the Queen for us."

Darya laughed delightedly and hugged Parvaneh. "I am so happy for you!" she exclaimed. "When will Master Arman speak to her?" Then her face fell and her arms dropped to her sides. "But does this mean you will be leaving the Queen's service?" she asked with a catch in her voice.

Parvaneh took hold of Darya's hands. "I hope not," she said gently. "Master Arman thinks not. He does not see why we cannot continue to work here for the King and Queen, as long as they agree to the arrangement."

Darya breathed a sigh of relief. "How wonderful that would be." She shook her head. "We were so wrong about Master Arman, were we not?" she asked Parvaneh. "We thought he hated the Queen and Master Mordechai, but he was only trying to protect the King, as he said."

Parvaneh nodded. "And now he is doing his best to help Majeed and me." She gazed sadly at Darya. "I wish he could help you, too." Darya lowered her eyes to the stones of the entryway as Parvaneh continued, "Will you speak to the Queen yourself, now that the troubles are past?"

Darya turned and began walking slowly toward the palace. "There is no reason to," she said sadly. "David has changed. We no longer talk. He barely even looks at me when he is in the Queen's chambers." She sighed. "I am a slave, Parvaneh. It is what I am and what I will be."

Parvaneh grabbed her arm. "But maybe that is why he has changed. Maybe he realizes Master Mordechai would never permit him to marry a slave. But if you were free...."

Darya stopped abruptly and faced her friend. "Free! And a Judean! And from a reputable family! I would need to be all those things for Master Mordechai to grant permission. You and I both know that."

Darya continued walking toward the Queen's chambers and Parvaneh trailed after her silently.

Thirty-One

Yet for all Darya's rational words, she lay awake on her mat that night with conflicting voices arguing back and forth in her head. One voice insisted that everything could change if she would only speak to the Queen about her freedom. But another countered that freedom would not be enough. She needed to be a Judean, not just someone who admired the Judeans and had learned about them. And she needed to be from a respectable family, not someone with a murky past who had no idea where she came from. And then there was a third voice—the worst of the three—that kept reminding her that David no longer spoke to her and tried not to look at her, and that he often seemed pained even to be in the same room with her.

A small sob escaped Darya's lips and she brushed tears from her cheeks. *Face the facts!* she chided herself silently, taking a long, shaky breath. *You are a slave. David is lost to you.*

But the first voice would not be silenced. It kept telling her that nothing would happen if she did not make it happen; that gaining her freedom might change things; that she should at least beg the Queen to hear her out and give her guidance. *You can trust the Queen*, the voice insisted. *You know she cares for you. You know she will advise you well.*

Darya grew calm and lay still. The voice had convinced her. She would approach the Queen and follow her counsel.

∞

She spent the next day waiting for an opportune moment to speak to the Queen. But the morning was too busy. A spate of new delegations arrived with requests from Judeans for assistance to rebuild damaged homes and businesses. Master Mordechai was in attendance with David at his side, of course, and Darya felt physical pain in her chest as she watched David position himself so that he would not be facing her.

Ignore it, the voice in her head admonished her. *Just find a moment to speak to the Queen.*

Queen Esther took her lunch in the garden with Artaxerxes and his nursemaids. She held the child on her lap and helped him examine a butterfly that had alighted on a flowering shrub near the dining table. Then she handed him a glittery golden ball and smiled as he tossed it around the garden.

Darya hoped the afternoon would be quieter, but messengers arrived with tidings about the capture of more attackers. The Queen and Master Mordechai took some time to peruse the lists of prisoners carefully.

At length, the Queen raised her head and looked pointedly at Darya and Parvaneh. "Your Master Behrooz is on this list," she said quietly, and both girls gasped. "Since he was part of Haman's inner circle," the Queen continued, "he has been brought to Susa to be imprisoned here until his trial."

Darya looked at Parvaneh and knew they were both thinking the same thing. Even though they had wanted Behrooz to be captured and imprisoned, they did not want him anywhere nearby. With his wily ways and sinister smile, even in prison he felt like a threat.

∞

Darya lay on her mat that night worrying about Behrooz, and frustrated that there had been no opportunity to speak to the Queen. She was determined to speak to her in the morning, but with the first light, a steady stream of petitioners and officials began filling the Queen's anteroom again. The Queen sat on a gilded chair on a raised dais in her audience hall, her guard Hasach at her side. She was beginning to look exhausted from all the days of meetings and audiences, but she listened to each supplicant intently, her entire attention focused on the person before her.

From her position near the wall of the chamber with Parvaneh, Darya noticed how Queen Esther inclined her head toward each speaker. "She wants them to be able to keep their voices low," she whispered to Parvaneh with admiration. "She is trying to give them privacy when they make their requests."

The girls watched as person after person came before the Queen, sometimes singly, sometimes in groups, and occasionally an entire family made homeless by the fighting.

Children with frightened eyes clung to their mother's skirt as their father begged the Queen for the assistance that she, of course, granted. After their audience, all were directed to the anteroom again to take some refreshment before leaving the palace.

The morning wore on. Darya lost count of how many people had come before the Queen. One face began to blend into the next. Darya lost hope that there would be any opportunity for her to speak to the Queen even on this day. She began daydreaming that she was one of the petitioners in the anteroom and that it was her turn to make a request. She envisioned herself moving forward, saw the Queen inclining her head toward her, and imagined herself pouring out her heart. The reverie actually made her smile, but she was jolted back to reality when she suddenly realized that the Queen had turned her head away from an official standing before her and was looking toward Darya and Parvaneh. The official looked at the girls too, and seemed to be scrutinizing Parvaneh, especially. He was a short, stocky man with an unruly, graying beard, and when he and the Queen resumed their talk, he seemed to have a great deal to say. Finally, after looking at the girls once more, the Queen gave some quiet instructions to Hasach, who nodded and moved to the front of the dais.

"Attention, please," he called out in a voice loud enough to be heard in both the audience hall and the anteroom. "The Queen will resume hearing petitions later in the day.

All those waiting to speak to Her Majesty will be given food and drink and a comfortable place to wait."

And with that, Queen Esther rose from her chair, stepped down from the dais, and left the hall with Hasach and the stocky official. Darya and Parvaneh could only stare after her, bewildered.

∞

Two hours passed before the Queen returned to her chambers with Hasach, but without the official. She stood still for a moment, looking thoughtfully at Darya and Parvaneh, who were ready to be of service, but she did not resume her seat on the dais. Instead, she stepped out into her garden and sat on one of the benches, hands folded in her lap, while Hasach stood protectively nearby.

The girls could see the Queen gazing contemplatively at the grass, the trees, the flowers, the sky, then down at her hands. She even closed her eyes for a while, as though she were concentrating and wanted no distraction. At last, she raised her head, opened her eyes, and rose from the bench. She moved to the far end of the garden, where she sat at a small table as far as possible from the audience hall, and almost hidden from it by shrubbery. After a few minutes, Hasach stepped toward the doorway and motioned to Parvaneh to join the Queen. The girl glanced in confusion and some trepidation at Darya and hurried toward the table.

Darya stood near the doorway to the garden, wondering what could possibly be going on. Was this something about

Majeed? Had Master Arman spoken to the Queen, and was she now giving Parvaneh her decision? If so, something seemed very wrong. This did not seem like a happy occasion. And who was the mysterious stocky official who had spoken to the Queen at such length and stared at her and Parvaneh? Darya looked questioningly toward Hasach, who was standing guard midway between the doorway and the table where the Queen sat with Parvaneh. She hoped he would give her some clue as to what was happening, but he would not meet her gaze.

After what seemed like an endless wait, Parvaneh emerged from behind the shrubbery and walked slowly toward Darya. Her head was down and she hugged herself with her arms as though she were chilled, even though the sun shone warmly.

"What is it? What has happened?" Darya whispered, as her friend came closer.

Parvaneh stopped and raised her head, a dazed expression on her face. She looked as though she were about to say something, but her eyes filled with tears and she turned and hurried from the room.

Darya looked after her, dread rising in her chest. She wanted to chase after her, to learn what was wrong, to try to comfort her, but she heard Hasach calling her name. She faced him and saw him gesturing that it was her turn to go to the Queen. With foreboding, she made her way down the garden paths to the table behind the shrubbery.

Thirty-Two

"Sit down, Darya," Queen Esther said kindly, when she saw Darya standing awkwardly near the table.

Darya moved stiffly to comply. She had to breathe deeply to calm herself, and to keep reminding herself that this was her beloved Queen sitting before her, the woman whose counsel she so desperately craved.

Esther lowered her head and folded her hands on the table, as she had folded them on her lap earlier on the garden bench. But this time, Darya could see that her fingers were squeezed together tightly, and her jaw was clenched. She sat that way for long moments, while Darya grew more and more apprehensive about what she was going to hear.

At last, Esther raised her head and took a shaky breath. "Darya, you know I care about you," the Queen began, and Darya nodded. "Sometimes I think of you as a younger sister, rather than my servant," the Queen continued, and Darya felt a warm glow deep in her being. "I have never wanted you to be hurt, and I have always tried to protect you."

"I know that, My Queen, and I thank you for it," Darya murmured unsteadily, wondering fearfully where this was leading.

The Queen took another deep breath. "You saw the last official I was speaking to in the audience hall this morning." Darya nodded and the Queen continued, "He is the Warden in charge of the prison in Susa—the prison where the man Behrooz was taken."

Darya breathed in sharply. "Has he escaped?" she asked anxiously. "Is that why Parvaneh looked so upset?"

"No," the Queen replied. "Behrooz is still in prison." But strangely, her voice was not as soothing as her words. "He is in prison," the Queen repeated, "but he is trying to bargain his way out."

"How can he?" Darya cried. "Your Majesty, he was part of Master Haman's inner circle! He was always with him, even that morning after I read to the King when Master Haman sought permission to hang Master Mordechai!"

"We are all well aware of that," the Queen said softly. "But Behrooz is in possession of some information— some important information—that he knew I would want to have."

Darya pictured Behrooz as she had seen him through the years—in the captain's house, on the path near Master Arman's office, at the King's Gate near Master Mordechai's office, in the King's chambers—always there, always amassing information, always seeming to know what was important. She waited for the Queen to continue.

"That is why the Warden came to me this morning," the Queen said. "Behrooz bribed him so that the Warden would come to me and plead his case."

"How could he bribe him?" Darya exclaimed. "He is in prison. He has nothing."

The Queen shook her head. "He has no more riches," she said, "but he has a wife and a child. And even in prison, he is still master of his household." Her mouth twisted as though she had a sour taste on her tongue. "He offered his daughter in marriage to the Warden if the man would convince me to hear what Behrooz had to say."

"Is it done, then?" Darya asked. "Has Your Majesty granted him his freedom for his information? Is that why Parvaneh was so upset?"

The Queen looked down at her hands again, still clasped tightly on the table. "That is not exactly why she was so upset," she murmured. "You see, Parvaneh's mother never told her who her father was. He abandoned them when Parvaneh was born. He had wanted a son and had no use for a daughter at the time."

Darya stared at the Queen, trying to process her words. Parvaneh's father? What did Parvaneh's father have to do with this? No! Was the Queen saying that the awful Master Behrooz was Parvaneh's father? Images crowded into Darya's mind of the way Behrooz always acted as though he had some sort of claim on Jaleh and had a right to be where she was. Was this why Behrooz had wanted Jaleh to have a position in the palace—because his friend Kansbar could arrange for him to have entry to the palace grounds since he was her husband? That would give him the opportunity to connect with powerful people like Master Haman. Then

Darya thought of all the arguments and half-made threats between Jaleh and Behrooz, and the hateful way Behrooz had looked at Parvaneh and treated her. And now he had sold his daughter to gain his own freedom—sold her to the stocky, gray-bearded Warden. Darya pictured Parvaneh's tearful, dazed expression when she fled the Queen's chambers. "No," she whispered. "Please, no, Your Majesty. Please do not let this happen."

The Queen slowly shook her head. "It is the law of the land," she said softly. "A father has the right to do as he wishes." Then she added, almost as an afterthought, "Of course, Parvaneh could arrange to buy her freedom from the marriage if she had the money, and if the Warden agreed."

"She could buy her way out?" Darya questioned. "But Parvaneh does not have much money, nor does Jaleh." She propped her elbow on the table and leaned her forehead in her hand. "What is she to do? She wants so much to be with Majeed. Master Arman was supposed to speak to you about the match. She was so happy."

Darya felt devastated for her friend. To find out she had an evil father and was bound for life to an older man she did not even know … It was all too much. But suddenly, Darya had a thought. "What of all the coins and trinkets I earned with my scribe work?" she asked excitedly. "Your Majesty has been holding them for me for safekeeping. What if I give it all to Parvaneh to buy her freedom?"

The words hung in the soft garden air, and Queen Esther looked at Darya with an expression that the girl could not decipher. "Think of what you are offering," the Queen said. "I am well aware that you have been saving that money for yourself, and now you are offering to use it for Parvaneh. Is that what you truly want to do?"

Darya pictured David's face and felt as though her heart was being wrenched apart. She had been planning to talk to the Queen about her own freedom, and now she was negotiating Parvaneh's instead. She wanted to cry; she wanted to scream; but she pictured Parvaneh's face again and knew she could not let her lose her dream of being with Majeed. Parvaneh was her dearest friend. Darya knew she could not live with herself if she did not do all she could to try to help her.

"That is what I want to do, Your Majesty," Darya forced out in a choked voice. "Please help me buy Parvaneh's freedom."

Thirty-Three

The Queen sat back and contemplated Darya. Finally, she said, "You and Parvaneh are eighteen years old. Darya, do you think you would have offered to trade your freedom for hers six years ago when I first met you, when you were twelve?"

Darya thought back to her first weeks in the palace, to Parvaneh visiting her in the slave barracks and trying to protect her from Golnar. She nodded. "Yes," she said. "I think I would have, Your Majesty."

"And when you were eight years old?" the Queen questioned. "Do you think you would have done it then?"

Darya pictured herself lying on her mat on the floor of Jaleh's room in the captain's house, curled up with Parvaneh like a pair of kittens. "Yes," she said again. "I think I would have."

"And when you were five or six years old?" asked the Queen. "Then too?"

Darya thought back to when she was that young: to being terrified and sick in the dark box on the slave wagon; to being chained to the wall by the slave dealer; to being sold in the slave market. Her hand went to her neck involuntarily. She felt the old choking sensation, and the scar that had never completely faded. "My Queen, I did not know Parvaneh when I was five or six," she said hoarsely.

Queen Esther looked at her sadly. "And yet you traded your freedom for hers anyway," she said.

Darya stared at her. "I do not understand."

Esther sighed and sat back in her chair. "Darya, you have known me since you served me in the women's quarters. Am I living a life that I chose to lead?"

Darya's mouth dropped open in surprise and dismay at the unexpected and almost treasonous question. Fearfully, she glanced around the garden. "Please, Your Majesty. Take care. I do not know what to say."

"I am asking you for an honest answer," the Queen prodded her. "We are in the garden, away from curious eyes and ears, protected by my trusted Hasach. So answer me. Do you think this is the life I always wanted to lead?"

Darya pictured Esther shut away in her room in the women's quarters, reading her scrolls, not mixing with the other women, only dressing up for her meeting with the King when Hegai insisted. "No, Your Majesty," Darya whispered. "I do not think you ever wanted to be Queen." It suddenly struck Darya that perhaps Esther had always been so secretive in the hope that someone like Master Arman would turn her out of the palace because of it.

Esther's eyes seemed to probe into Darya. She asked, "If you do not think I ever wanted to be Queen, then why am I here?"

"You had no choice," Darya responded. "Young women were forced to come to the palace." She thought back to the young woman from Sardis, crying as she wrote home to her family, and all the other young women shut away in the women's quarters.

"True," the Queen said. "I had no choice. But what does that mean? Why do things happen to us in our lives? Why do we get to be where we are?"

Darya pictured Jaleh in the captain's kitchen all those years ago, frightening her when she had said sharply, "The *ahura* put you with that slave dealer for a reason, and they put you here for a reason, just like Parvaneh and I are here for a reason. They sent the captain to war, and they brought Behrooz here this morning—all for a reason. And we must all live up to it."

Darya looked at the Queen and said softly, "You became Queen for a reason."

Esther nodded. "Think about that," she murmured. "What if I had not become Queen? What might have happened to my people?"

Darya shuddered. "Are you saying that your life was sacrificed for theirs?"

"In a way, yes," Esther responded. "Oh, I am alive, and I live in luxury. But this is not the life I would have chosen to live. Just as you are not living the life you would have chosen. Your freedom was sacrificed ... for someone else."

Darya felt a prickling sensation on her scalp and down her back. "Please, My Queen. What are you not telling me?"

she whispered. "What information did Master Behrooz share with you?"

"I think it is becoming clear to you," the Queen responded. She stood up and beckoned to Darya to walk with her along the garden path. "Behrooz had no qualms about selling his daughter to gain his own freedom now, when she is eighteen."

Understanding flashed in Darya's mind. "So he would have had no qualms when she was five or six either. Is that what you are saying?"

The Queen nodded. "He was a gambler, and deeply in debt. He needed money to avoid becoming a debt slave himself, and he was ready to sell Parvaneh into slavery instead."

Darya felt her throat constrict. With difficulty she asked, "How were we traded? How did I become a slave in her place?"

"Who would have tried to protect her?" the Queen asked.

Darya stopped in her tracks and felt sick to her stomach. "Jaleh?" she questioned in a strangled voice. But she knew the answer. She pictured Jaleh always showering Parvaneh with gifts like ribbons and the butterfly shawl, letting her sleep late, pampering her, hugging her, kissing her, while Darya—the slave—was the frightened child who was chained to a wall like an animal and beaten by the captain's first housekeeper and shoved onto hot embers in the fireplace and slapped by Monir's aunt and bludgeoned almost to death by Golnar.

Blindly, Darya stumbled back to the table. She dropped into the chair and laid her head against the cool stone of the tabletop. She could make no sense of this. Jaleh was her protector; she treated her like a daughter; she let her sleep in her room; she gave Darya her first coin for her twelfth birthday; she nursed her back to health after Golnar's beating.

But Jaleh was the reason she was a slave. Jaleh was the one telling her to forget the dreams of the beautiful man and woman, and the playful little girls, and the delectable food, and the magical garden, and to thank the *ahura* for blotting out her past! Jaleh was not her protector! She had turned Darya into Parvaneh's protector! So that was where her name had come from—the name the slave dealer had told to the captain and Monir—the name that Darya had not recognized as her own. Jaleh had named her Darya: protector. At least that was an honest act. But what was her real name, Darya wondered? It was lost, along with her past and her family and the life she was supposed to have led.

She gritted her teeth and heard animal sounds emerging from her throat as she tried to stifle the sobs and screams she wanted to let loose on the world. She covered her head with her hands and pressed it against the table, trying to shut out the truth and the deception.

She did not know how much time elapsed before she felt the Queen gently patting her back. Slowly, Darya raised her head and squinted into the sun-filled day. Somehow, she had thought it would have turned cloudy and thunderous to match how she was feeling. Exhausted, she sat up in her chair and gazed dully at the table.

The Queen sat down across from her again. "I know you are in terrible pain right now," she said gently, "but you must remember what you told me earlier—that you would willingly have exchanged your freedom for Parvaneh's when you were twelve and even eight years old." She took Darya's hand and squeezed it. "Your love for Parvaneh must not change because of the sins of her father and mother."

Darya nodded mechanically, but she did not really know if she would ever be able to feel close to Parvaneh again, even though none of this was her fault.

"And now you must hear the full truth, as far as I know it," the Queen said, "since I was not completely honest with you before for reasons that will become clear."

Darya looked at the Queen with trepidation and listened as she explained that Jaleh had kidnapped the child of a family visiting her employers in Pasargadae, the beautiful city that had been King Cyrus's capital, where he was now buried. Pasargadae was a few days' travel from Persepolis, where the visiting family was from. Jaleh handed over the child to slave dealers in place of Parvaneh. She regretted her actions almost immediately, but could not undo them without endangering Parvaneh and herself.

"She promised herself that she would follow the kidnapped child wherever she was taken, and do her best to protect her in her new life as a slave," the Queen said. "That is how she came to be in Susa, ready to be hired by your captain when he was in need of a new housekeeper a few months after you arrived there. She knew it would have been safer for her to stay away from you, but she wanted to protect you if she could."

Darya understood that the Queen was trying to preserve any good feeling Darya might still have for Jaleh, but all she could feel was pain and betrayal. The Queen did capture Darya's attention when she said, "Parvaneh will not be forced to marry the Warden. The laws of the land do not permit such a thing, and you need not redeem her with your savings." She looked at Darya meaningfully. "I told you she had to buy her freedom because I wanted you to realize that you would willingly give up your own freedom for hers."

Darya nodded mutely, and the Queen continued, "Behrooz is being granted his freedom in return for the information he shared with me, but he is also being banished from the Empire. You and Parvaneh will never see him again, and need have no fear of him."

"Thank you," Darya murmured with relief, but she stiffened when the Queen added, "Jaleh, however, is now in prison awaiting trial for the kidnapping." The Queen looked at Darya with compassion. "She is a broken woman, Darya—overcome with remorse and eager to make amends any way she can. We will take that into account at her trial, along with the fact that she tried to protect you when she could." Darya nodded numbly as the Queen continued. "She told us the names of her employers in Pasargadae, but unfortunately, she never knew the names of the child's parents who were visiting them, only that they were from Persepolis. And so, Darya, we are able to restore your freedom, but so far, we cannot tell you who you really are. I will send investigators to Pasargadae and Persepolis immediately to see what they can find out, but it will take some time for them to travel there, to make inquiries, and to send us word of what they find."

Darya said nothing. She felt as though she had no energy to move or even think, and she certainly had no energy to hope to learn who her family was and then possibly have her hopes dashed. Eventually, the Queen rose and turned toward her chambers. "Sit here as long as you like," she said kindly. "When you are ready, we will talk about your new life as a free person."

Thirty-Four

Darya was never entirely sure how she spent the rest of that day, or the evening and night that followed. She knew she stayed in the garden until it began to grow dark, then she left through the small garden gate and wandered the palace paths. She paid no heed to where she was walking or whom she passed along the way, not really caring where she was or what might happen to her.

Eventually she grew hungry and tired, but she was loath to return to the Queen's apartments, where she might see Parvaneh. She avoided the stables too, where Nasim might want to ask her questions about Jaleh and Behrooz. Then, remembering that Jaleh was now in a jail cell and no longer working in the kitchens, she wandered over there. Feeling like a beggar, she asked a serving girl for a plate of food.

Finding a place to sleep was her next concern, until she thought of the women's quarters. Hegai was still in charge, and he permitted her to enter without question. The dimly lit, quiet hall was balm for her troubled spirit, rekindling pleasant memories of her days as a scribe and her nights sleeping next to the cascading waters with Parvaneh. Hegai found her a sleeping mat and some cushions, and she sank tiredly to the ground near the central fountain, leaned her back against it, and let its musical flow lull her to sleep.

In the morning, she knew she had to return to the Queen's apartments. After all, she was still in the Queen's service, even if she was no longer a slave. The thought brought her up short, and she spent a few moments examining how this made her feel. How was she different now from what she had been yesterday before the Queen's revelations? Did she hold her head higher? Was her step firmer? Was she somehow more intelligent or quick-witted? What exactly did this word "freedom" mean?

She was still pondering this when she entered the Queen's apartments and saw Parvaneh in the anteroom. She looked tired and bedraggled, her eyes red and her cheeks puffy from crying. When she saw Darya, she looked as though she wanted to sink into the floor, and the realization struck Darya like a blow just how difficult all this must be for Parvaneh: to find out all at once that her father was a rebel capable of selling his own child, her mother was a kidnapper, and her closest friend had been living the life of a slave that had been destined for Parvaneh herself.

Darya wanted to hold onto her anger and hurt. She wanted to direct it at Parvaneh, because Jaleh and Behrooz were not there to give her release. But all the years of friendship came flooding back—all the days and nights spent together, the work shared, the confidences exchanged, the support given—and she knew she could not hold a grudge against Parvaneh. The Queen had been right. Parvaneh was innocent, and Darya would always be her protector. Slowly, Darya walked toward her friend and put her arms around her, and the girls clung together silently because no words could express what they were feeling.

∞

The Queen spent the morning seeing petitioners again, but took her lunch at the far table in the garden and invited Darya and Parvaneh to join her.

"Master Arman spoke to me two days ago," the Queen said to Parvaneh, after serving girls had placed food before them. "Your situation has changed since then," she said gently. "It is no longer your mother making this request for you, and so I must ask you directly—are you and the soldier Majeed still seeking permission to marry?"

"Yes, My Queen," Parvaneh said almost inaudibly, looking down at the table. "He sent word to me last night. In spite of—" Her lips trembled and she stopped and pressed them together. Then she took a calming breath and said, "In spite of everything, he would still like to marry me, and I would like to marry him."

"Then you have our blessing," the Queen said, and Parvaneh smiled wanly. "The King and I agree that you may continue in your positions as palace guard and handmaiden for as long as it suits you, although you will need to take lodgings outside the palace walls, in Susa."

Parvaneh's smile broadened and Darya squeezed her hand in joy. "Thank you, Your Majesty," Parvaneh said. "We will continue to serve you well."

The Queen nodded in satisfaction and turned her attention to Darya. "Have you been able to give any thought to your future?" the Queen asked her.

Quietly, Darya said, "Unless the royal investigators are successful, I have no other home and no other family. If it pleases Your Majesty, I hope to continue to serve you."

The Queen nodded again and said, "It pleases me." She added, "The investigators have been dispatched but, as I told you, it could be weeks until we know anything."

The three ate in silence, surrounded by the soft, fragrant air of the garden. Darya's thoughts turned back to David. She wanted so much finally to tell the Queen about her feelings for him, but she could not think of how to express what she wanted to say. She knew this was her opportunity, and the lunch hour was slipping by, but she continued to eat silently, her eyes on her plate.

At last, just as the Queen was preparing to rise to return to the audience hall, Parvaneh burst out, "Your Majesty! Darya has been craving your advice on an important matter, but she cannot find the courage to speak to you about it!"

Darya's face reddened as the Queen tried to suppress a smile and turned to her. "You would like my advice?"

Darya nodded. "Yes, My Queen." But she still could not find the words. At length, stumbling and stuttering, she said, "About David … I am free now … I have been studying about the Judeans … I still do not know my family, but I know they were not slaves … Do you think it is possible? Do you think Master Mordechai might…?" Darya finally gave up and sank into silence. She looked pleadingly at the Queen, hoping she had understood something of what Darya had been trying to say.

The Queen cleared her throat. "You are hoping that now that you are free, Master Mordechai might consider you as a possible match for David. Is that what you were trying to tell me?"

"Yes, Your Majesty," Darya said gratefully.

"Master Mordechai has always considered you a fine person, as do I," the Queen said gently. "He has always admired your intelligence and how capable you are. And it has been obvious to everyone that you and David are … friends … and that you have been interested in learning about the Judeans and our beliefs. Everyone also knows that you worked tirelessly to help us through our troubled times."

"Thank you, Your Majesty," Darya murmured, but somehow the Queen's words were not comforting. They sounded like a speech she had prepared that was leading up to something that Darya did not want to hear.

"However," the Queen went on, "during the troubles, as you know, delegations of Judeans visited the palace." The Queen hesitated, and a note of compassion crept into her voice as she said, "Darya, a merchant from Persepolis met with David and proposed a match for him that was accepted by Master Mordechai."

Darya heard Parvaneh gasp, and felt as though she had been punched in the stomach. She was in pain and found it difficult to breathe as the Queen continued speaking.

"The merchant and his family will travel to Susa so that David and the young woman can meet. They are expected to arrive within two weeks, and if all goes as planned—meaning if David and the young woman agree—there will be a betrothal."

Darya could not speak. She could only nod.

"I am sorry, Darya," the Queen said softly. "I wish for your sake it could have been otherwise."

Thirty-Five

Mysteries come clear. Questions are answered. Situations change. Life goes on. The phrases spooled through Darya's mind like yarn being wound on a spindle. Large parts of her history had been revealed, she understood much of what had happened to her, she had gained her freedom, and she had learned why David's attitude toward her had changed. But where did that leave her? What was there to hope for now, and to dream about?

Darya fulfilled her duties in the Queen's chambers as capably as ever, but she moved from one task to the next like a sleepwalker, separate from the active, waking world around her of feelings and friendships and plans. She had to smother her feelings in order to stifle the pain attached to them. She had to separate from friendships because of the plans that were now associated with them—plans about betrothals and weddings and dwellings—plans that would never be part of her own life, this new life of freedom that she had so desired.

She knew she should encourage Parvaneh to discuss her arrangements for the future. After all, who else was there for Parvaneh to talk to, with her mother in prison awaiting trial? But she knew her interest would be false and her smile would be forced, and she had no room in her life for any more dishonesty. She also knew she should seek out David to congratulate him on his good fortune, and let him congratulate her on her freedom. But, again, she knew that anything she said and did would be a sham. And so she continued to sleepwalk through her days, watching the morning shadows disappear at noon and lengthen again toward evening, knowing that just as the sun was traveling through its arc, the Queen's investigators were traveling to Pasargadae and Persepolis, and the young woman chosen for David was making her way to the palace.

And then, suddenly, toward evening at the end of the week, there was David in the anteroom, with a message for the Queen from Master Mordechai. Darya was startled by the intensity of her reaction. Her legs grew weak, making her grab a chair back for support. She could not take her eyes from his face, even though she knew she should lower them demurely. And she could not stop smiling at him, in spite of the fact that he was not smiling in return. After glancing at Darya, Parvaneh quickly slipped out of the room, mumbling that she would go find the Queen, and the two were left alone.

The silence lengthened uncomfortably until David cleared his throat and said, "Congratulations on your freedom." He gave a small, mirthless laugh. "I never thought something good could come from dealings with a man like Behrooz."

Darya nodded. "It is strange how things happen, how there is some sort of plan in the world, like the war on the Judeans bringing the merchant from Persepolis to the palace." She took a steadying breath. "Congratulations on your betrothal."

"Not quite," he countered. "After all, Leah and I have not even met each other."

Leah. The name filled every corner of Darya's mind. Leah, the daughter of the merchant from Persepolis—the girl who resembled Darya that Monir had written about in her letters. Another strange coincidence.

"I am sure it will work out for you," Darya said. "I have heard from my former mistress, Monir, that Leah is from a fine family. Master Mordechai would only choose wisely and carefully for you."

David nodded. "I trust Master Mordechai." He hesitated, then added quickly, "I hope that eventually the Queen will choose wisely and carefully for you too, now that you are free." She could see he was debating whether to say something more. Finally he added awkwardly, "I always intended … I decided a long time ago, Darya, that if you had not gained your freedom, I was going to buy it for you … and…." He was obviously going to say even more, but he stopped and looked down at the patterned carpet.

"Thank you," she said quietly into the uncomfortable silence and dropped her eyes to her hands, still gripping the chair-back. Then she looked toward the doorway, hoping to see Parvaneh returning to lead David to the Queen, but the doorway stood empty.

"Darya," David said so softly that it was almost like the sound of a deep breath. Her eyes flew back to him. He said, "I want you to understand … I must explain…." He ran his hand across his eyes and looked at her miserably. Then he cleared his throat and began again. "Darya, my parents fell ill when I was only a child. Master Mordechai promised them that he would take me in, raise me as a Judean, educate me in our laws and customs, provide me with a livelihood … and find me a Judean bride who would help me keep their names alive through the generations."

He sat down and clasped his hands in front of him in agitation. "Darya," he went on. "I was going to buy your freedom. I was going to tell Master Mordechai of all your questions about our religion, all your interest. I was going to tell him that I thought you might want to become a Judean. I was going to convince him that you were the kind of person who could fulfill my parents' wishes." He looked at her sadly. "But then the troubles began, and it felt like there were two circles in the world: the Judeans in one circle and everyone else outside … some attacking us, some helping us, but still outside."

The circles, Darya thought. She remembered that she had felt them, too: the Judeans praying in the square, all the planning and preparation in the Queen's chambers— the inner circle and the outer circle—and she had been on the outside.

"So when Leah's father came to Susa, and Master Mordechai told me about the proposed match, it felt right," David continued. "It felt like this was what my parents wanted for me—to marry someone from the inner circle, someone raised in the way I had been, someone who understood the laws and the traditions ... and what it felt like to be persecuted for your beliefs."

I tried to understand! Darya cried out in her mind. *I tried to learn about the laws and traditions. And I certainly am aware of what it feels like to be persecuted.* But she understood what David was saying, and she understood why Mordechai had to fulfill his promise and find the kind of bride he was sure David's parents would have wanted for him.

"I am sorry," David said gently. "I know I should not be telling you this ... not now ... not with Leah on her way here ... but I thought you deserved to know. You are very special, Darya. I would have been proud to have you as my wife."

My wife. Darya savored the words even as tears filled her eyes. But there was no more to say, and she was relieved when Parvaneh returned to tell David that the Queen was ready to see him.

Thirty-Six

Leah and her parents arrived the following week, late one evening, and settled into lodgings in the city. The next morning, a post rider arrived with a report from the Queen's investigators.

"Jaleh's employers moved away from Pasargadae years ago," the Queen told Darya, as the girl helped her dress. "The investigators are trying to track them down. They are also questioning residents of both Pasargadae and Persepolis, to see if anyone remembers anything about the kidnapping. When we meet with Leah and her family today, we will ask them if they know anything about it."

Darya nodded mutely, and the Queen added carefully, "Darya, Jaleh's trial has begun." Darya was silent and the Queen continued, "I want you to know that I am asking for clemency for her, as I told you I would, because of how she is cooperating and because of how remorseful she is."

Darya remained silent, but then she nodded and said softly, "I do not want her to hang." She looked at the Queen sadly. "What she did was a terrible thing ... but I look at Your Majesty and Artaxerxes ... and I think of Jaleh's love for Parvaneh ... and Parvaneh being taken from her...." She shook her head and could not go on.

"I am sorry, Darya," the Queen said gently. "This must all be so difficult for you."

Darya only shrugged. Yes, it was awful to think about the kidnapping, and the frustration of the investigation, and Jaleh's trial, but today it was even more distressing for her to think about Leah and her parents actually being in Susa.

Following their night's rest, they were all to join the Queen for a festive luncheon prepared according to Judean laws and traditions, after which David and Leah would be given some time to become acquainted. Darya knew she did not want to be in attendance on the Queen during the luncheon or afterwards. She went about her morning duties with her jaw clenched and muscles tensed, trying to decide how to ask that the Queen excuse her, but of course the Queen anticipated her request and paved the way.

"I am sure you would prefer not to be at today's luncheon," the Queen commented almost casually as Darya helped her cut flowers in the garden and arrange bouquets for the table. "We will let you know if Leah's family has any information for you."

Darya exhaled and felt herself relax. "Thank you, My Queen," she murmured.

"Where would you like to spend the time?" The Queen smiled. "After all, you are a free young woman with the afternoon to yourself. What would you like to do?"

Darya's mind was blank. What would she like to do, she wondered, now that she had the right to choose for herself? She tried to picture the free women she had seen through the years, and realized that she had very little experience of that world. She had grown up serving in a household run by a housekeeper, then moved into service in the palace. She pictured the young women in the women's quarters, painting, playing instruments, embroidering, watching entertainment, and then she pictured the young Esther, reading at her desk in her room.

"I would love to spend the day in the palace library," Darya exclaimed with a smile. "To have time to browse, to read whatever catches my eye, to explore...."

Esther shared her smile, fully understanding Darya's pleasure and eagerness. "Go," she said. "Enjoy."

∞

The library was large and dusty and quiet, the walls lined with shelves, and the shelves piled high with scrolls of papyrus and parchment, many in protective tubes, and each with an identifying clay tag hanging down.

Darya strolled through the room like a visitor on holiday, running her hand through the tags and making them clink and clatter like wind chimes. She read inscriptions on tags, lifted scrolls off their shelves, and unrolled a few to read their first few lines. Finally, she dropped an armful of choices onto a reading table and settled into a chair. She rummaged through the tags and shook her head ruefully. Fully half the scrolls she had chosen were about the Judeans: their history, their religion, and their recent troubles in the Empire.

Strange, she thought to herself. *Even with no hope of being with David, I am still interested in learning about his people.* She unrolled a scroll and immersed herself in a description of the Temple that had stood in Jerusalem until Queen Vashti's grandfather, King Nebuchadnezzar, had destroyed it. Then she compared the description with a second scroll that detailed the plans for rebuilding the Temple—plans that had been approved by King Cyrus.

She remembered reading months ago about how the rebuilding was suspended because of complaints by the Samaritans, who were newer residents in Judea, but she had never noticed the stark difference between the two descriptions. The first Temple was gilded and grand, while the second was only a poor cousin of the original. It did not seem as though the Judeans were asking for much, and yet even this modest request was being contested. Why, she wondered? Why so much suspicion and jealousy and mistrust in the world? And why so much persecution and pain—like her own?

She laid down the scrolls and gazed at the long shafts of sunlight angling through the high library windows. They were almost vertical, so it was near noon, just about the time that Leah and her parents would be arriving at the palace. They were special visitors, so Darya knew they would not be kept waiting at the King's Gate. Their carriage would roll through the entry maze, past Master Mordechai's office, and enter the King's garden that so enthralled guests the first time they saw it. Then they would ride through the *paradaisia* of blooms to the Queen's apartments, where they would be ushered into her glorious garden, to find the luncheon laid out magnificently.

Darya rested her head on her arms on the library table. She wanted to continue reading scrolls to keep her mind fastened elsewhere, but her thoughts kept returning to David meeting Leah: the lovely, well-bred Judean that Master Mordechai had chosen for him, the girl who had grown up loved and protected by her parents in Persepolis, rather than being kidnapped and sold into slavery in Pasargadae.

It occurred to Darya that David would most likely continue to work for Master Mordechai after his marriage, which meant that she would see him often, and Leah as well. How could she cope with that? She would need to leave. She would wait until the Queen's investigators completed their work—which she doubted would yield any useful information—and then, because of her newfound freedom, she would have the right to go. But where? If they did not find her family, the world would be just a large, hollow, empty void for her, with no welcoming lights beckoning from any windows.

A great weariness came over her, and she closed her eyes. This so-called blessing of freedom lay heavy on her spirit. With no one to order her to be somewhere or do something, she had to learn to make her own plans and decisions—even though she had no desire to plan the lonely life that stretched endlessly before her or to decide where she would live it. She only wanted to sleep until this miserable afternoon waned, and then she wanted to sleep more, until David and Leah were wed, and then more and more and more….

She did not know how long she lay with her head on the table before she heard a step nearby. She raised her head, feeling dazed and groggy. The shafts of sunlight were slanted in the opposite direction from before; it was past noon, but not very late in the day. She looked around to see who had made the sound she had heard, and saw a veiled woman standing quietly on the other side of the table.

Darya jumped up, causing her head to spin. She grabbed the table to steady herself, then lowered her head respectfully. "How may I serve you, My Lady?" she asked.

"No … no … please sit," the woman said. "I would like to speak with you." Her voice was soft and youthful, and she moved gracefully to take a seat opposite Darya at the table.

Hesitantly, Darya sat down again. The woman's veil was too thick for her face to be seen clearly, but Darya could tell that she was young, and obviously well bred.

"You are … Darya?" the woman asked in a tentative voice.

"Yes, My Lady," Darya replied, taken aback that the woman knew her name.

"Please," the woman said softly. "Do not call me that. My name is Leah."

Darya stiffened and inhaled sharply. *Monir's friend*, she thought, her heart sinking. *The young woman chosen for David.* She cleared her throat and forced herself to say calmly, "Congratulations on your betrothal."

Leah hesitated, then said, "I am not betrothed—at least not yet."

"Then … then why are you here?" Darya could not stop herself from asking. "Forgive me, but should you not be at your luncheon … or with David … getting to know him?" All at once, she sat up straight and stared at the veiled figure. "Did the Queen send you? Are you here because you have information for me about the kidnapping?"

"Yes," Leah said slowly. "I have information for you about the kidnapping … and more."

Darya's heart raced. She could not catch her breath. She clutched the edge of the table with shaking hands. "Please," she whispered. "Tell me. Do you know my family? Do they still live in Persepolis?"

"Yes," Leah said gently. "I know them—your parents and your sister. They still live in Persepolis."

"Parents? Sister?" Darya echoed. Tears welled up in her eyes. Her long-ago dreams lit up her mind: the beautiful man and woman, the playful little girls, the fragrant flowers, the delectable food arranged on painted dishes. It had all been real.

Darya covered her face with her hands. "Do you know my name?" she asked in a muffled voice.

There was no response, and slowly Darya lowered her hands to look at Leah questioningly.

"Your name is Rachel," Leah said at last.

"Rachel," Darya repeated, as though tasting the name on her tongue. "A Judean name."

Leah nodded. "Yes. You are Judean."

Like the Queen, Darya thought in wonder. *And David.* She wished for time to explore how this made her feel, but there was so much more she thirsted to know.

"What is my sister's name?" she asked.

Slowly, Leah lifted her veil. "You already know my name," she said in a choked voice.

Darya stared at the young woman before her. Her face was identical to Darya's; she could have been looking at an image of herself in a mirror. Darya sat frozen. This was more than she could comprehend. Her body and mind refused to react. Then Leah gently reached across the table and, as though moving on their own, Darya's hands reached to grasp her sister's—tightly—as though they would never let go.

"We used to hold hands all the time, did we not?" Darya whispered, as an avalanche of memories engulfed her. Leah nodded, and Darya said, "We did everything together, even sleeping, curled up like a pair of kittens."

Leah nodded again, tears streaming down her face. "All these years ... a part of me was missing. We were in that garden together, then suddenly you were gone. Did you feel that way too?"

Darya stared down at their clasped hands. "For me ... everything was missing. I was sick for a very long time, and afterwards, nothing was clear anymore.... I did not know who I was, I did not know where I came from, I had no understandable memories. There was only emptiness ... and fear."

"How did you survive?" Leah asked tearfully. "At least I had our parents; I had a home; I had friends and a community. But you—the Queen told us you were sold into slavery!"

Darya thought back to the slave caravan, the metal collar, the slave market, and her tears. "There were people who cared about me," she said quietly. "Monir, and my friend Parvaneh, and the Queen, and ... and others." She knew she could not have survived without Jaleh, but she was still too hurt to add her to the list. And she knew she should have mentioned David, but not if he was to be her sister's betrothed.

Leah squeezed her hands and said, "There is so much for us to talk about—so much I want to know—but we must go back to the luncheon. Our parents thought it would be best for me to come here first. They did not want to overwhelm you. But they can hardly contain themselves. They are so eager to welcome you back into the family."

"Our parents," Darya echoed softly. "I have parents."

Leah smiled. "Yes. You have parents, and a sister, and a home, and a community—and there will even be a betrothal."

The girls let go of each other's hands and began to rise from the table, but slowly Darya sat down again.

"What is it?" Leah asked with concern. "You look frightened."

Darya looked away from her, wondering how to explain. She felt foolish and childish. Everything she had ever dreamed about was real, and yet she was afraid to embrace it.

"Please," Leah said. "Speak to me. Let me help."

Darya took a long, shaky breath, but did not face her sister. "For as long as I can remember, I have lived the life of a slave," she murmured. "How do ... I do not know how.... How do I suddenly learn how to be free?"

Leah started to speak, but Darya raised her hand to stop her. "I have lived the life of an orphan," she whispered. "How do I learn to be a daughter?" Her hands began to tremble; she clasped them tightly on the table to still them. "I have been alone in the world. How do I learn to be a sister?" Her voice began to shake and she struggled to control it. "I never knew where I belonged. How do I learn to be a Judean?"

Leah took her seat again, and they sat across from each other in silence. Darya let her hands drop into her lap. Her shoulders sagged in exhaustion. The silence lengthened, until slowly Leah began to speak.

"Darya," she said softly. "I think I should still call you that, until you are more comfortable with your real name." Darya shrugged as Leah continued. "I did not ... I am so sorry.... None of us realized how difficult this would be for you."

Leah stopped and the silence lengthened again until she said, "Darya, you had to be strong to survive what happened to you. We were told that your name means 'protector,' and that you always tried to help people.

We were told you even tried to protect the Queen!" She stopped again, as though she were searching for the right words. "Darya, you will not be facing this new life alone. You will be surrounded by people who care for you and will help you; people who want to be strong for you; people who want to be *your* protectors—our parents, and me ... and of course, David."

Darya finally looked up and smiled wanly. "Thank you for that," she said, "but I do not think I will see too much of you and David after you are married. You will be here in the palace, and I will most likely be in Persepolis."

Leah stared at her. "After David and I are married?" she repeated in surprise. "Why would you say that?"

It was Darya's turn to stare. "Because of the betrothal, of course."

Leah's bewildered expression slowly transitioned into a smile. "I was not speaking of *my* betrothal," she explained. "I was speaking of *yours*!" And at Darya's confusion, Leah continued, "As soon as the Queen and Master Mordechai and David saw me, they realized who you were. And as soon as they realized who you were, they understood whose betrothal would take place today!"

Darya shook her head in disbelief and sat rooted to her chair.

"Please, Darya," Leah said. "Trust us. None of us will betray you or abandon you. We will give you all the time you need to learn to live the life you were always supposed to lead."

Leah rose from the table and stood looking down at her sister. "Please, Darya," she repeated. "Trust us."

After a long while, Darya rose as well. Leah smiled at her encouragingly, and the sisters clasped hands as they used to do long ago. Together they walked through the library, sometimes through shadow and sometimes through slanted shafts of sunlight, moving toward the life waiting for them in the Queen's garden.

Author's Notes

The Book of Esther in the Bible tells us that seven handmaidens were assigned to each of the women brought to the palace to meet King Xerxes. I began to wonder who these girls were, and that is how the story of *The Seventh Handmaiden* was born. Darya and Parvaneh are fictional characters, but the Persian lifestyle and events described in their story are as accurate as I could make them.

Historical fiction makes history come alive, but it's important for readers to know what is real and what is fiction. The non-fictional characters in this novel are taken from histories written about the Persian Empire and from the Book of Esther.

Historical figures who appear in the story are the Persian kings, Cyrus the Great, Cambyses, Darius I, Xerxes, and Artaxerxes; the Persian queen, Amestris; and King Nebuchadnezzar of Babylon.

People taken from the Book of Esther are King Xerxes, Queen Vashti, Prime Minister Haman, Queen Esther, her relative Mordechai, the courtiers Bigthan and Teresh, and the servants Hegai, Charbonah and Hasach.

The Book of Esther was written in Persian and Hebrew. The Hebrew version is called the Megillah, which means "scroll." Like most ancient documents, it was written on sheets of papyrus or animal skin that were attached in a row. The long, completed document was rolled up into a scroll to make it easy to carry or store. The names in the Megillah were also written in Hebrew. The king is Achashverosh (also spelled Ahasuerus), which is very similar to what his name sounds like in Persian—Chashavaarasha. The name Xerxes used in this book is what the Greeks called this king in their histories. Since the Greeks eventually conquered the Persian Empire, destroying most Persian records, and since winners write the histories, it is mainly Greek versions of names and events that have come down to us through the centuries. That is why I used Greek names when there was a choice: for example, the prophet of the Zoroastrian religion is named Zarathustra in Persian. But I used Zoroaster in this book, which is the Greek version of his name.

I also had to make choices about when and how certain events in the book took place, if different historians interpreted them in different ways. There are conflicting views about when and how long the Persian Empire existed. I chose to use the dates accepted by the majority of historians: 550 BCE–330BCE. For interpretations of how and why certain things happened, I was greatly influenced by the book *Esther, Ruth, Jonah, Deciphered*, by Stephen Gabriel Rosenberg. Dr. Rosenberg neatly blends the events of the Megillah with Persian history described by ancient Greek historians and others. As with the histories of any people and time period, not all historians explain them in the same way. Dr. Rosenberg's explanations made the most sense to me, so I used them in the novel.

King Xerxes ruled for between 14 and 21 years, according to different historians. He was not well liked, and his reign ended abruptly when he was assassinated by courtiers like Bigthan and Teresh. Queen Esther lived out her life in the palace. As I have her tell Darya in the novel, it was probably not the life she would have chosen for herself, but being queen enabled her to save her people.

Historians are not in agreement about the name and identity of the next king. The version I prefer is that Esther's son ascended the throne and that his name was Artaxerxes. I prefer this version because the king who followed Xerxes allowed the Jews to build their Second Temple in Jerusalem. The building of the Temple had been promised by Cyrus the Great, but was put on hold by Darius I and Xerxes. It seems logical to me that a son of Esther might be the one to finally allow the project to be completed.

The Megillah is read each year when Jews celebrate the Purim holiday. The word "Purim" means "lots," as in the word "lottery". Haman is described using lots to decide when to attack the Jews. This means that he threw down dice, or a handful of pebbles or sticks marked with various dates. He believed that his gods chose the date that came up in the lottery and therefore his plan would be successful.

But Purim is a joyous holiday for the Jews because they were saved from Haman's destructive plan. People wear costumes and masks to hide their identity, like Queen Esther hid hers. They make noise to drown out Haman's name when it is mentioned in the Megillah. And they spread good cheer by exchanging gift baskets of food, sharing a festive meal, and distributing gifts to the poor.

The Persian Empire truly was tolerant, which was unusual in the ancient world. As long as conquered people accepted their rule, the Persians granted them freedom to live their lives and practice their religions. This policy was established by Cyrus the Great, a progressive leader who also realized that ruling this way would make his subjects more cooperative and less likely to rebel.

There was slavery in the empire, but the Persians did not act like the Romans, whose empire rose a few centuries later. They did not enslave entire populations of conquered people. Instead, they often made them citizens and paid them for their labor. They also allowed women more freedom than was permitted in many other societies of the time. However, Persian kings were absolute monarchs, with the power of life and death over their subjects. They could be extremely cruel to those who crossed them, and they were described as backward barbarians by Greek historians. But, remember again, the winners write the history, and Greek historians were almost certainly biased; after all, they were writing about hated enemies that they had conquered.

Glossary

Aba: Aramaic word for Dad.

Ahura: In the Zoroastrian religion, the group of god-like beings who are helpful and good.

Ahura Mazda: The chief god in the Zoroastrian religion.

Angarium: The Persian postal service set up by King Darius I. It was the best in the ancient world. Swift riders carried messages from one postal station to another, where they were immediately transferred to fresh horses and riders. Many centuries later, in the 1800s, the American Pony Express mail service was set up the same way.

Apadena: The massive royal audience hall in the palace in Susa. Its roof was held up by 36 magnificently carved, tall columns.

Aramaic: The common language used in Persia, Mesopotamia, and Israel in ancient times. (Mesopotamia was a region centered in modern-day Iraq.) Each region also used other languages, like Persian and Hebrew. Aramaic was written with a simple alphabet based on the 22-letter Phoenician alphabet. The Phoenician alphabet also became the basis for the one we use today.

Babylon: A grand city on the Euphrates River in central Mesopotamia. In the Bible, it is called Babel or Bavel, and it is the site of the story of the Tower of Babel. It is located southwest of modern Baghdad in Iraq. After it was conquered by the Persians in ancient times, it became a major city in the Persian Empire. Because of its excellent location, it was taken over by one group of people after another as a base to expand their power.

Babylonia: The name of two different empires ruled by the kings of Babylon. The first empire was built by the Amorite people who had settled in the city of Babylon; the second was built by the Chaldean people who settled there hundreds of years later.

Cin (pronounced "chin"): Ancient name for China.

Daeva: In the Zoroastrian religion, the group of god-like beings who are hurtful and evil.

Darics: Coins in a money system established by King Darius I of Persia and named after him. Using the same type of money throughout the Persian Empire made it easier to trade and build the economy.

Ema: Aramaic word for Mom.

Great Sea: Ancient name for the Mediterranean Sea.

Hieroglyphics: Complicated alphabet of more than 1,000 picture symbols, invented and used in Egypt.

Iran: The modern name of Persia. In 1935, encouraged by Nazi Germany, the Persian government decided to change the name of their country to Iran.

Judea/Judeans: After the reign of King Solomon, the ancient Kingdom of Israel split into two parts. The north continued to be called Israel. The south became known as Judah. It was named for its ruling tribe, who were the descendants of Judah, one of the 12 sons of the Jewish Patriarch, Jacob. Greek and Roman conquerors called the Kingdom of Judah "Judea." Its people were known as "Judeans." This term was eventually shortened to become the word "Jew."

Kidaris and **Kulah**: Types of men's hats in ancient Persia. Some men wore headbands instead of hats. Turbans were not worn in Persia until centuries later.

Magi: The priests of the Zoroastrian religion.

Nebuchadnezzar: The greatest king of the second Babylonian Empire, established by the Chaldean people. He conquered Judea (the southern part of Israel), destroyed the First Temple of the Jews in Jerusalem, and exiled the Jews to Babylon.

Papyrus: A reed plant that grows along the Nile River in Egypt. It was, and still is, used to create many products, including the first type of paper. The word "paper" comes from "papyrus."

Paradaisia: Magnificent formal gardens that surrounded the palaces of the Persian kings. They were so beautiful that the word "paradise" comes from "paradaisia."

Parchment: A smooth and thin type of material to write on, made from calfskin, goatskin, or sheepskin.

Pasargadae: The original capital city of the Persian Empire. It is the site of the tomb of Cyrus the Great, first emperor of Persia.

Persepolis: The main capital city of the Persian Empire. Susa and Ecbatana were the two other capitals. Since the empire was so large, it was ruled from more than one capital and from several principal cities. Persepolis was the most elaborate capital. It was where religious festivals were held.

Qanat, Kariz, Ab Anbar: Qanats are ancient underground tunnels that carry water many miles from the mountains to the dry lowlands of Iran, which used to be called Persia. Many qanats are still in use today. The kariz is a trench that branches off from the qanat to carry the water to other areas. The ab anbar is a private reservoir to collect water brought by qanats.

Silk Road: The ancient trading routes from the countries of the Far East, like China and Japan, to Persia and Mesopotamia in the Middle East. Silk and spices were the most popular products, and silk gave the routes their name.

Susa: One of the three major capital cities of the Persian Empire, along with Persepolis and Ecbatana. Located in today's southern Iran, it was used as a business capital. In the Book of Esther, it is called Shushan.

Wars with Greece: Called the Persian Wars, these were a series of uprisings, battles, and two wars fought between the Persians and the Greeks in the fifth century BCE. They were fighting for control of Ionia (in today's Turkey), on the western coast of the Persian Empire, and eventually for control of Greece itself. Since Persia was so much larger and more powerful than Greece, it was expected to win. However, the Greeks won both wars because of better military strategies. Even so, Persia remained a powerful empire until 200 years later, when the Greeks, under Alexander the Great, finally conquered it.

Wedge Writing: Known as Cuneiform, this is a complicated alphabet of more than 700 wedge-shaped symbols, invented and used in Mesopotamia. Ancient Persian was written with Cuneiform letters.

Wind-catcher: A tower that is like a chimney built onto a house. It was meant to catch the slightest breeze and funnel it into the house to make it cooler.

Xerxes: The Greek name for the Persian king who ruled during the second Persian War. In the Book of Esther, he is called Achashverosh and marries the Jewish girl Esther. In Persian, his name sounds something like Chashavaarasha.

Zoroastrianism: One of the main religions practiced by the Persians in ancient times. Its prophet was called Zoroaster by the Greeks and Zarathustra by the Persians. The religion is still practiced today.